1283

W9-BZF-025

$/25

ONE OF THOSE WOMEN...

As a plastic surgeon, Nina Field had found satisfaction in treating the scarred and the desperately unhappy people whose lives were changed by her operations. But as she sat in her room at the United States Hospital in Saigon, she was disturbed by the number of useless cosmetic jobs she had to do, which took her away from the patients who needed her. . . .

And then there was Sergeant Dave Lawlor, whom she loved and who might not come back to her—for any of a number of reasons. . . .

Nina was one of those who wait for their men to come back from war. And her presence so close to the battlefield didn't make things any easier. . . .

For
SAM ALLALOUF

WOMEN OF THE GREEN BERETS

BY RAND MICHAELS

LANCER BOOKS • NEW YORK

A LANCER BOOK • 1967

WOMEN OF THE GREEN BERETS

LANCER BOOKS, INC. • 185 MADISON AVENUE • NEW YORK, N.Y. 10016

PART ONE

One

AMBUSH DUTY is supposed to be pretty easy.

That's what the men tell each other when they exchange the trade talk of war. Suppose some officer in the conning tower at base should hear, say, a pair of crickets rubbing their noses together. That man gets in touch with HQ, which sends a company down to investigate. (There may be a little exaggeration in that part about the crickets, but the new sound-detection equipment can let a trained man hear jungle sounds from far away, and that gives him a chance to get up plenty of false alarms.) Every man in the team takes his M-16, an ammo pouch, a grenade issue, a long knife, an entrenching tool, and a water canteen. It's possible that some newspaper correspondent will go along, so that he can see what war is like at first hand and print what he sees in the newspapers. There's likely to be a photographer too, carrying his own weight in camera equipment and not so much as a single grenade.

A chopper takes this crew over the area, and they drop and sniff around for trouble. As a rule there's nothing doing, but a company lieutenant is as likely as not to order his men to dig in and wait around in case Victor Charlie shows up. If Victor Charlie doesn't make the scene, which is what usually happens, each man has got through one more night of his year-long tour, and it's been peaceful.

Every so often, though, Victor Charlie does drop around.

When that happens, all hell breaks loose.

Matt Colbert was in charge of the team. He had made

captain only a few days ago, and he was still taking pleasure in the promotion and the feeling of power that went with it. He was top man, and it was his job to take care of the others who were under him and to kill as many of the enemy as he could manage and to make sure he got the most out of his men.

He was the sort of man the Special Forces consider worth finding. Twenty-seven years old, muscular, shrewd, and a fellow who wouldn't short his men on anything. He'd had three civilian careers, all in minor spots where he'd had to take orders from other people, and he'd flubbed every one of them. After an argument with Evelyn, he'd enlisted and tried out for Green Beret training. From that first day in Fort Bragg, he'd known pretty damn well that he had found the one career he really wanted.

He supposed that the career had helped to save his marriage. The good deal was that he didn't have to see her too often and he liked her more and more when they did manage to get some time together. She liked the arrangement too, he was sure.

Matt had been reading a letter from Evelyn just before the call came through. Evelyn had got it into her head that she wanted to come to Vietnam and see him. She said she was making arrangements for the trip, that is, seeing "the right people," and buying things, and so on. Evelyn believed from the bottom of her heart that the right people could fix everything from a passport to an incurable brain tumor.

He wanted to see her, heaven knew, but he was going to write and say that she ought to think twice about coming over to Saigon. Then the call came, and it wiped everything else out of his mind.

He made a point out of talking cheerfully to the men before the chopper started to rev up. They got inside finally, Matt going first and Sergeant Dave Lawlor after him. It took the company past the outer perimeter of the Phan Khe base camp and partway into thick, leafy jungle.

6

There was a clearing with logs and brush in it, a clearing that looked suicidal as a jumping-off point but was a sure bet to show not any trace of Victor Charlie's cute traps. The pilot hovered above that point. As company leader, Matt made the jump first. He did it proudly, and the pride lasted even after he had landed harder than expected and massaged his kneecaps tenderly to make sure he hadn't cracked them. From the minute he got to his feet, he started clearing logs for the next man, to make the jump a little easier. Lawlor reached him in a minute and then joined the log-clearing. By the time Fentriss and Hubbard arrived, Matt was peering through the October night for any trace of Charlie. Nothing. It was going to be one of those moonlit, peaceful nights, he half-hoped, in which his men wouldn't have a hard time.

Dave Lawlor, at his side, was saying, "I can take first watch with the dingus, Captain, if that's all right."

The dingus was a sniperscope. While one man watched and listened, everybody else in the company could snooze up a storm.

"I'll make assignments when the time comes, Sergeant," Matt said stiffly.

He heard a grunt behind him and turned to see if one of the men might have run into any trouble. That was the moment when all hell broke loose.

Gunfire thundered beyond the clearing, and then a bright ball of flame appeared where the chopper had been. There was a scream, probably from the trapped pilot, but the sound of an explosion cut the scream sharply. The pieces of chopper fell swiftly, lighting the terrain and giving Charlie a clear view. Grenades, flares, and streaks of automatic rifle fire pierced the night's gloom as Matt and his men scrambled for cover.

Lawlor, who was next to Matt, asked quietly, "A direct charge, sir?"

"I'm not going to risk one man more than I have to." He considered the terrain, then said, "Come on with me. We're going after that gunner."

7

The machine-gun stutter could be heard as Matt led the way, crawling on hands and knees to the point beyond the clearing from which he felt sure the sounds were coming. The stutter of that machine gun in Vietcong hands was enough to set Matt's teeth on edge, even though not one hit had been scored as far as he could tell.

He fired at the sound as he came closer. Expecting Lawlor to do the same, he was surprised to hear the man shouting, instead. He was shouting in the Bru language, repeating one word again and again, but Matt couldn't make out what the word was.

And then he thought the fire had changed direction. There was a sudden high-pitched screaming and the jungle floor shivered lightly under the footsteps of running men. They ran toward the trees, where Matt could see them in a momentary burst of flare light.

His men must have seen the running VCs too. They started firing. The helpless VC tried to change direction, but it was too late. One of Matt's grenades disposed of three men, and coolly accurate gunfire took most of the others to their Maker. Every VC in this group would call out and throw up his hands before dying, almost as if they had all agreed in advance on some way to signal their friends that the end had come.

The machine gunner still hadn't been taken, but the arc of a flare showed him running toward the clearing, machine gun in hand. His lips moved as he shouted, and a stream of spittle flowed between them as he fired savagely at his former comrades.

When Matt realized what was happening, his response was automatic and not reasoned out. The man with a machine gun was a native who had been fighting with the VC. Before anything else could be done, before that deadly stutter could possibly be turned against his men, Matt threw one grenade. The machine-gun fire stopped.

The after-battle silence tore at his nerves. He whirled around on Dave Lawlor.

"What the hell were you doing over there?"

"I talk a little Bru, sir, and I called him a traitor," Lawlor said quietly. "The combination of my shouting at him and your firing in his direction must have made him lose his head. He thought one of his boys was doing it, and he started shooting. Sure could move like a bolt of lightning, sir."

"I wouldn't think it would make him blow his top so completely, unless . . ." Matt stopped. "Sergeant, find out about our casualties, if any, and make sure a chopper has been clued to come after us."

"Yes, sir."

Matt advanced toward the point where the machine gunner had been killed. The man's body was still intact except for the head, which Matt's grenade had blown off, but the gun, which was supposed to be at least ten times more sturdy, had been smashed to pieces by the impact.

Matt's pencil flashlight showed that the man had been wearing black pajamas, as most VCs did. The left breast pocket bulged slightly. Matt tapped it from outside, then picked a tree branch that had fallen and used it against the pocket the way he would have used a brush. He heard papers spatter down to earth. By the light of a pencil flash, Matt saw at least fifty piaster notes.

"What the hell!" he called out, then whirled around as Dave Lawlor came closer.

Lawlor said softly, "He'd never have so many p-notes if he wasn't working for us. No wonder he turned tiger so fast."

Matt remembered how the first bullets had missed his men steadily and how he'd put it down to bad aim on some VC's part.

"Just a minute," he said. "What about our casualties?"

"Fentriss and Jordan, sir."

"Wounded?"

"Both dead, sir."

Matt winced. Fentriss had been a quiet man but an effective one. Jordan had been colored and the best-coordinated man, in Matt's opinion, at the Phan Khe base.

9

"We'll take our bodies back," Matt said, and pointed downward. "Him, too."

"Sir?"

"He worked for us, and he ought to have a decent burial."

"Yes, sir," Lawlor said, adding heavily, "There's bound to be a ruckus about this back at the base."

"You're probably right, Sergeant. I'll have to take good care to win it."

Two choppers, one from the medical-evacuation team, got to the scene in less than half an hour. Three dead bodies were taken on board the Green Giant chopper. No soldier made any remark about the Vietnamese body, but Matt could sense their disapproval without a word having to be said.

The return to base took a short time. Matt's Viet counterpart pursed his lips tautly when he heard about the extra body.

Matt said stubbornly, "I've been told to take care of the men fighting under me, and either those instructions mean something or they're completely hypocritical."

"This man wasn't fighting under you, Captain Colbert," the counterpart said, his body rigid. "I'm—hum!—glad you're so considerate about the men whose rank isn't as high as yours."

"Thank you, sir."

"I take it, then, that you'll have no objections to arranging for the burial."

"I'll attend to it, sir."

"Good," the Viet Captain said, smiling for the first time since the matter had been brought up.

Matt went back to his tent for a few hours of well-earned rest and spent a large chunk of the next day arranging for the burial. The mayor and village chiefs of Phan Khe refused to take the body at first, but the payment of a few piasters to each of the chiefs made them change their minds. The mayor was swept along by the tide of opinion.

10

A coffin of wooden boards was carried from the exact geographical center of Phan Khe out to the burial grounds. A Buddhist priest sprinkled water on the coffin, and it was interred with its contents.

Colonel Esterbrook personally thanked the village mayor for his cooperation in the matter. The mayor replied that cooperating with the United States was always an honor.

Sergeant Lawlor happened to find out what took place later on with the body of the dead Vietnamese. It happened that the mayor saw some of the village chiefs with their bribe money and drew the correct conclusion. He called in some of the village's young Turks, so to speak, and told them truthfully that the body was headless. The young Turks all knew that a body without a head was that of a man who could never find happiness in the hereafter and whose spirit was doomed to wander forever and ever. The young Turks were upset about it and decided to take action on the very next night.

Four of them showed up at the cemetery, dug up the coffin, and carried it out to jungle territory. The coffin was opened, and the body tumbled out of it and was left to rot in the sun.

When Lawlor heard about it he said that it was a perfect example of the way things got done in this country. "Figure it out for yourself," he added to his informant, a sergeant named Hubbard. "The Viets said okay to a request of ours, Ken. Right?"

Ken Hubbard nodded.

"They actually did what we asked them, which shows that we're getting good cooperation around here. Right? They did bury the guy, like we wanted."

"I suppose so; yes."

"And the lieutenant proved that the U.S. Special Forces have got principles of their own and that we look after the ones who fight for us. Isn't that so?"

"In a way, I suppose." —

"In every way, Ken. And what's the result? Everybody

11

cooperates with everybody else, everybody is satisfied, and nothing has been done. If that isn't Vietnam in a nutshell, Ken, I'd like to know what the hell else is."

"I suppose so," Ken Hubbard said again. He didn't actually feel sure whether it was so or not, but it never hurt to play along with Dave Lawlor.

Two

EVELYN COLBERT, Matt's wife, reached Saigon at the end of October, anxious to see her husband; but she soon began to wonder if she wanted to see him right away.

She'd never have arrived at the capital of South Vietnam if she hadn't haunted the U.S. Embassy at Hong Kong and signed a number of forms that said she was giving up practically every right of an American citizen. She couldn't have cared less. The embassy had to follow up on certain procedures that made sense to them, and she had decided a little while ago that she had to see Matt again and do it soon.

She was a small blond with full cheeks and a figure that was likely to go to pieces soon after she became thirty. She didn't eat or drink or smoke too much. She was a shrewd, sharp-eyed girl who hadn't had any wool pulled over her eyes for as long as she could remember.

As a girl in Pocatello she had wanted to be a model but had soon realized that she didn't have the face or features to carry it off. She became assistant to the manager of a modeling agency, and it tickled her when she decided that models were probably the stupidest creatures ever put on earth. She'd been reasonably happy, with a decent career and a boyfriend who was beginning to think about the advantages of getting married. She would take him around for dinner at the houses of her married friends, and he'd sigh a little when it came time to say good night. Evelyn supposed that the hard work of going home alone after a pleasant night had taken more men to the altar than any other factor.

He was getting his nerve up to propose, as Evelyn remembered it, on the night they were scheduled to have dinner with Francine and Harvey. That was a bad night. Francine was at Harvey's throat for most of the evening, and when the two of them weren't actually arguing she would sometimes call him "dear" with the kind of inflection that made it plain she actually meant to say, "Drop dead, you bastard!"

Evelyn's boyfriend hadn't proposed after that particular set-to, and he never had another chance. She was introduced to Matt Colbert several days later, and from that time on her life had been like something put into a dice box and rattled around all the time.

Matt had been a door-to-door salesman in those days, and his big complaint was that the front office always gave him leads that weren't worth the paper they were written on. In the few months they knew each other before getting married, he switched jobs twice. In the second place, the front office gave him solid leads, but they insisted he clock in to work every day and that he wear red ties. In the third place the front office didn't push him around, but the leads they gave him turned out to be worth even less than they had been in the first outfit.

In one way or another, Matthew Colbert was going to be his own boss or blow a gasket trying.

Evelyn had no doubt that marriage and a family and responsibilities would tame her man, but marriage by itself seemed to take its own sweet time doing it. He put in a short spell as a carnival barker and then took a franchise in a department store. He ought to have done well behind a store counter, Evelyn thought, but there wasn't much business.

"The place is like a desert," Matt said about it once, long after he had decided to give it up. "I had plenty of chances to read books and do some thinking."

He decided on getting into the army before the army got hold of him. Evelyn agreed that if the army didn't steady her man, nothing would do it. Heaven knew how he'd found his way to the Special Forces operation, but it soon turned out that the man who hated taking or-

14

ders from anybody else was able to give them as if he'd never done anything else in his life. And he seemed to have been born with the knowledge that a person in command had to look out for the people who were under him.

Evelyn was so glad her husband had found his true career that she resigned herself to it even though it was not the one she'd have picked for him. She lived in a housing development in North Carolina, a trailer camp in Florida, and a small hotel in Hong Kong. Matt used to slip over to Hong Kong on rest-and-recreation trips, but Evelyn couldn't get a job there, and time dragged. She hoped she'd be useful in Saigon and at the same time get a little closer to her husband and spend more time with him when he was free.

It would have made perfect sense for somebody like Evelyn Colbert in any city of the world except the one she had just reached.

Sightseeing was a waste of time, she was sure, so she got into a cab at the Ton San Nhut airport and didn't look out again until the driver stopped and opened the door at her left.

She was in an Oriental city that didn't look any different from Hong Kong. Cabs, cars, and pedicabs crawled through traffic. Women walked with food purchases carried in twin buckets that dangled from bamboo poles across their shoulders. Boys in their early teens were hawking pet monkeys, cricket cages, old newspapers, and cigarette lighters. There was a smell of fish in the air.

Evelyn registered at the Pinot Hotel on Kam Roh Street and wasn't surprised to find that the hotel service was good and that a few piaster notes here and there got her the things she needed. There was a perfectly acceptable dining room in the place, but the main course at dinner was a kind of bluefish she didn't much care for, along with sweet-tasting seeds arranged in a circle on the plate.

She was staying close to the hotel, because Matt had

told her he'd be there in the evening. All her arrangements had been made a few weeks in advance, and Matt had written that he expected he'd be spending at least forty-eight hours with her.

By nine o'clock he hadn't shown up.

At half-past nine she went down to the desk in order to find out if there had been any communication from Captain Colbert. There hadn't been. She said she'd be in the hotel all night and wanted to know as soon as he came in or there was a phone call. The clerk promised he'd take care of everything.

At half-past ten she came to the desk again. There was a different clerk back of the counter, and he knew nothing about Evelyn's problem. He did look inside a desk drawer, though, and came up with a letter that looked as if it had been delivered a few hours ago. Evelyn turned away angrily from the desk and neatly opened the envelope with two long fingernails.

Dear:
Sorry I can't be there to welcome you to the big city. I've been given a new assignment that looks interesting and might even be fruitful. I hope I'll see you in a week or so. Please be careful.
                                                    Matt

Evelyn folded the letter and put it inside her seashell purse. There was nothing she could do about the delay, and she saw no profit in getting upset.

She went up to her room and tried to sleep, but the loudest thunder she'd ever heard kept her from it. She decided to wait it out, but it wouldn't stop and she didn't hear the sounds of heavy rain. Although her blinds were drawn, she could see pinkish-white colors on the other side of them. She realized that she was listening to the sounds of war, attack or defense. She didn't know which, but she wasn't going to lie here and wait for the worst to happen.

No doubt there was some sort of shelter in this hotel.

16

The most sensible thing to do was to go there and wait till the hellish sounds came to a halt. There wasn't any telephone in her room, so she hurried downstairs to the clerk's desk. She had dressed herself quickly, and it surprised her to see the clerk dozing.

"Where's the shelter?"

"Madame?" He spoke English with a French accent.

"The shelter." She had to shout. "The Vietcong must be pretty close."

The clerk smiled tiredly. "They are always close, madame, and the Americans are always blasting away at night. One becomes used to the sound."

Evelyn nodded slowly. If anybody heard them often enough, the noises would simply become part of the atmosphere, like jet planes streaking through residential districts back in the States.

"I'll need earplugs if I'm to have any chance at a night's rest."

No plugs were available, the clerk said, but they showed up as if by magic when she gave the clerk ten piaster notes. The only trouble with the darned things was simply that they couldn't shut out the vibrations made by mortars pounding into the jungles around Saigon. She sat up, put on a plain dress and low-heeled shoes, and went down to the lobby again. Not a creature was in sight except for the clerk, but soft lights could be seen back of the partly curtained door to the bar. She walked inside.

The place was half-filled. A small, dark man came over to her, drink in hand. "Would you like something, Miss?"

"Yes. I'd like you to leave me alone if you don't mind."

He looked shrewdly at her. "Got the screaming jumps?"

"Yes, if you must know."

"Blame it all on ignorance. I can cure you in a few minutes. . . . No, you don't have to pull back. I'm not so new at the business of getting along with women that I have to talk about sex as soon as I meet one. Sex isn't what I had in mind at the moment, oddly enough."

"I won't take any cure that involves drinking."

17

"No need for that."

"And the cure won't pay off too well, I'm afraid." She held up her left hand so he could see the wedding ring.

He was going to say something else, but he stopped himself and said, "Do you want the cure or not?"

"All right."

He led her up the rickety elevator to the top floor and then toward half a dozen wooden stops. She hesitated.

"Why are we going on the roof?"

"Don't worry. There's absolutely no danger."

She stepped onto the roof with a feeling that she was taking her life into her hands. Screens had been put up so it would be impossible to jump or fall off, though, and a dozen other people were standing around and staring at a view that was in a class by itself. There would be flashes of orange laced with black, and every so often a light would shine as it moved down across trees and leaves in the distance. Deafening as the noise had seemed when she heard it for the first time, she found that it was even possible to talk up here if she moved her lips slowly.

Her escort had promoted a pair of binoculars from another man on the roof, and he let her see the shells thunder into the jungle. He tapped her on the shoulder so she'd look at him, and when she had obliged he said, "They do it all the time late at night, automatically, or the Cong would be all over this town."

It was such a beautiful sight that Evelyn found herself pressing toward the screen so she could see more clearly and muttering under her breath when the wire mesh played hob with any part of her view. She sighed when it came time to give back the binoculars, but in some respects the whole view was more interesting.

After twenty-five minutes she felt she had seen as much of it as she'd ever want to, though, and turned away. Her escort followed, the nearly empty drinking glass in his hand.

Evelyn turned. "Thanks very much for calming my nerves. I was afraid that the Vietcong had attacked."

"If they did that, they'd probably kill too many of their own," he said somberly. "Let me buy you a drink. You look like somebody who could use one."

"I'm afraid you're right."

She looked more closely at her benefactor when the two of them were back at the bar. He was maybe a couple of inches taller than she had guessed and about thirty-one or -two years old at the limit. His face was small, his chin stubborn, his ears set back tightly against his head. She was very much aware of his sharp eyes.

"I'd like a White Russian, please," she said.

He nodded and came back with it, as well as a black martini for himself. There was what looked like dried seaweed in her glass, and he told her that he'd got a piece of Zubrowka from an empty bottle of Polish Bison vodka. It was a delicacy, he hinted. Instead of fazing him by ordering what she had expected would be a hard-to-get drink in Saigon, she had found her ace trumped and she had to look pleased at the sight of dry seaweed in her glass.

"What are you doing in this town?" she asked lazily.

"I'm in procurement."

"That's an all-purpose word."

"Not in South Vietnam it isn't," he said seriously. "The U.S. government is trying to build this country from the ground up. My job is to find out what's needed and get it out here fast as possible, and at the best prices."

"Best for the government?"

"No, for business. When a government goes to war, big-business interests lay in wait to make good money, and always do."

"You mean you're selling defective materials?"

"God, no. Believe me, business can do well enough by selling merchandise that works. The profit is pretty damn high."

"You've relieved my mind again."

19

She wondered lazily whether she'd give in to him. It'd be a quick contact, a night's fun that wouldn't do any harm. She hadn't been with any other man since she got married and wondered what it would be like now that it was going to be so simple to manage. Wouldn't it be funny-strange if Matt's staying away on this one night made her go through with it? Or if she fell for this man and ended up asking Matt for a divorce?

She never knew exactly how much time was spent in conversation, but she did have a couple of drinks after the first one. There was a pleasant glow inside her as Will Redmond—she had found out his name by this time, of course—walked with her up to the room. She wasn't absolutely sure whether or not she'd let him inside.

She was smiling lightly when she turned to him, trying to guess how he'd approach the subject of what he really wanted.

"Thank you for a wonderful evening," he said pleasantly. "I'm only sorry it has to end so soon."

"It's half-past three."

"Yes." Will smiled. "I suppose you've decided against fighting me off, Evelyn, should I suggest spending the night together?"

She waited, having made up her mind only that it would be a waste of time to duel with words.

"Nobody has to know except us, of course," he went on, adding moodily, "and we may be two people too many."

He raised his left hand. For the first time she saw the wedding ring he wore. "I've got a wife and I haven't had her very long," he added. "It's damn foolish to say no to a good-looking woman, and I guess I'll always hate myself for it."

She was angry enough to tell him, "I certainly hope so."

But when she was alone in the room and had locked the door on herself, she burst out laughing. When the fit was over and she was getting ready for sleep, she realized that the night's little adventure had left its mark on her thinking.

20

She loved her husband, heaven knew, but she'd have been interested to find out what she would feel like with another man. Just once it would be interesting. Just once, now that she didn't see Matt nearly as often as she'd like.

Three

DAVE LAWLOR was a man with some highly developed skills. He could murder another human being with a gun or several different kinds of knife or a chop with the underside of either hand or with two fingers used in a certain deft way. He didn't get any pleasure out of killing, but the SF had sent him out to this country to help get rid of Vietcong in one way or another. He was going to do that job as well as he knew how.

He had already finished a twelve-month tour and had put in for another, not so much because he enjoyed the job but because he'd rather be an important cog out here than a third assistant nitpicker in a candy factory, or whatever in hell job he might land when he got back to Stateside.

The war had been pretty tame on this tour, mainly because Charlie would get into his hidey-hole and not come out unless he was absolutely sure he'd win. Even when Charlie had the edge, in some situations he wasn't sure to come out.

The whole war had become routine, as far as he was concerned. A month in the field, then three days of R and R with Nina, and that was it.

He was feeling down-at-the-mouth when Captain Colbert called him in for some talk. Lawlor accepted Matt Colbert as his superior officer and knew that the guy looked out for his team, but Colbert was one of those people who would rather play it safe than stick his neck out. As far as Lawlor was concerned, the captain's general attitude about taking risks was the wrong one with which to fight this war.

Colbert was looking calm and satisfied about something or other when he gestured Dave into his tent. "Do you know the base at Tam Hung?" he asked for openers.

"Never been there, sir," Dave said.

"Your luck is going to change, Lawlor. I've been put in charge of an A team to go up there, and I'm making you part of it."

"Thanks very much, sir—I hope."

"Tam Hung is near the Cambodian border, Sergeant, and we're likely to see more action than even you might care for."

"Don't get me wrong, sir. I'm not all hopped up to get my head handed to me or anything like that. It's just that we all came out here to do a job, and we'd better do it."

"We came out here for two jobs, Sergeant, and I'm hoping we can get a hook into the second one now."

"We can't do very much in the way of pacification, sir, if Charlie comes along and smashes everything to pieces."

"We have to try, though, and keep Charlie from doing damage." Colbert pursed his lips. "We shove off tonight, which is going to make a dent in some plans of mine, and maybe yours, too."

"Yes, sir."

"You told me once that your girlfriend is a plastic surgeon in Saigon. When you write to her, be sure to put the blame on me and you'll get yourself off the hook."

"It'll be all right, sir, but thanks." Dave Lawlor grinned, showing wet white teeth in a sun-scorched face. His good humor had come back at the prospect of a change. "Like you said, sir, she's a plastic surgeon. When anything happens that she doesn't like, she can put a good face on it."

"Just for that, Sergeant, you can get the hell out of my tent."

In the next few hours Dave Lawlor found out that Colbert had picked himself a strong team. Lieutenant Ablett was going to be on the job to backstop any wrong plays. Ken Hubbard would be part of the A team, too, and so would a number of other people who were good at what they did. The twelve men who were going to spend such a lot of time with each other up in the tail end of hell had better get along together, and with Hubbard and Ablett around the chances were pretty good that the team was going to work out as a strong unit.

The team went by Flying Fortress to Ban Me Thuot, and the rest of the way in three trucks. Most of the driving was done along a one-lane highway flanked by tea plantations with silky-looking bushes that could've hidden dozens of Charlies. Lawlor kept both eyes out for any signs of Charlie, but it looked like a waste of effort until they got to a fork in the highway, one end leading to a mud road.

There was a village close by, and some half a dozen burly Montagnard tribesmen, each of them looking as if he could eat a wooden board with nails and all, came out to greet the new arrivals. Instead of moving out, Colbert signaled the drivers not to make tracks and gestured for Lawlor to keep an eye out for trouble. Some Montagnard women came to see the soldiers, too, and since every one of them was bare-breasted it wasn't the easiest job for Lawlor to keep both eyes peeled for any signs of trouble. He was Dave Lawlor, a man with a job to get done, and he did the damn job. But he grinned from ear to ear when the trucks moved again.

The A team wasn't going to have the Tam Hung base to itself, of course. They were sharing it with a Vietnamese counterpart team and a company of Civil Defense irregulars made up almost entirely of men from the Teh sect. Four other CIDG companies were stationed like chessmen on a board along the outposts that hugged the Cambodian border, according to the briefing that Matt Colbert gave his team, and about five hundred Popular Forces militiamen were in the district too.

When the fighting got underway it was going to be tough, the way Dave Lawlor liked it. The only trouble was that the fighting never seemed to get underway.

"I can't take much more of this crap," Lawlor muttered as he was setting out claymore mines along the outer defense perimeter of the base in the evening. "Nothing happens."

Corporal Overby, who was a demolition expert, sighed. He was more patient and stolid than the sergeant and felt that there was no pleasing some people.

"What the hell are you groaning about?" Lawlor demanded. "Once more like that, and I'll ream you."

"I was just—"

Lawlor's temper broke into a thousand pieces. He whirled on the inoffensive Overby and threw a fist, aiming low. He was so angry that he missed as the level-headed corporal jumped to one side.

Lieutenant Ablett had seen what happened, and he gave Lawlor a chewing-out he wouldn't forget for a long time. It wasn't the end of the matter, either. Colbert called him in to the sandbag-rimmed log bunker that he and his Vietnamese counterpart took turns in using as the base command post.

"What's this about a brawl with Overby?" the captain demanded, looking up sharply as soon as Dave walked in. "I want to tell you a fact of life you might not know too well, Sergeant. SF was organized in the early fifties as a guerrilla operation. We were trained in destructive skills —hand-to-hand fighting, demolition, and so forth. The picture has changed now. We still use our destructive skills, but the emphasis has switched to our helping rebuild this country."

"Yes, sir."

"People like you, Sergeant, find the fighting much easier than pacification. In fighting the issue is clear—will you survive? In pacification work, you're up against the individual quirks of the Vietnamese, their slowness and their liking for doing things in a roundabout way. In fact, pacification is damn hard work."

"I know it, sir."

Colbert kept looking calmly at the sergeant. "I sup-

25

pose you feel you've got to let off some steam, so I'll tell you what I'm willing to do. I have no objections to your fighting Overby, provided he gets a fair chance at you."

"Sir?"

"You and him will fight in front of the balance of the team, and the fighting will be by Queensbury rules," Colbert said slowly. "In fact, I'm going to referee the bout myself, Sergeant, and I might as well let you know that I'm betting on Overby."

Lawlor smiled. "I'd like a piece of that action, sir."

"You've got it—no, wait! A referee shouldn't show partiality, Sergeant, so I won't make any bets. But if I were betting, my money would be on Overby."

"Sir, you'd probably be the only one in camp who feels like that."

"It'll make for a better fight when Overby scores his upset," Matt Colbert said. "That'll be all, Sergeant."

The team tent had been picked as the place where the fight was going to happen, and cots had been pushed to one side so they could be used for seats. A square had been marked up in the dirt, a square about as big as a boxing ring. Dave and Overby were using gym shorts instead of regulation trunks. Colbert had dug up boxing gloves from somewhere and he apportioned them to each man without taking account of handsizes.

The fighters needed to have seconds, of course. Dave picked Lieutenant Ablett at first, but Colbert decided against the lieutenant working one side of the ring. Dave picked Ken Hubbard instead. The lean, rawboned Kentuckian was a good choice.

There had been some betting, Dave had heard, and the notion of anybody putting money on Overby in a fight against Dave Lawlor made the sergeant laugh.

But his laughter stopped during the first round of the fight. Dave came out of his corner with a tiger's snarl, ready to draw first blood and get rid of his frustrations of the last couple of weeks. He ran into a punch from

26

Overby that nearly stopped him cold. He'd never forget the way he suddenly started staggering around as if looking for ropes he could grab in order to keep himself standing.

The other men had seen how much damage the punch had done him, so Dave wheeled around and charged into Overby. He kept close to the corporal, wanting a chance to clinch and do some damage in a small flurry of punches. Overby needed only to touch him, it seemed, and Dave's whole system felt as if it were torn apart inside him.

Between rounds, as Ken Hubbard massaged him skillfully, he whispered, "You all right?"

"That son of a bitch has got a punch like a mule."

Hubbard laughed mirthlessly. "You giving up?"

"Hell, no."

"If I think you've seen enough action, I'll throw in the towel."

"Try it and I'll come after you next."

The second round was as bad as the one before it. Overby waited for him to get closer and then lashed out. He got in only two punches during the round, but he didn't need more.

Between rounds this time, Lawlor asked, "Where does he get the power?"

"Damned if I know," Hubbard said. "Try to relax so I can smear some of this gook on you."

The fight was scheduled to go for six rounds and by the fourth Dave was hardly able to drag himself to the chair he was using between rounds. Colbert came over to him and looked down gravely.

"Are you feeling all right, Sergeant?"

"Uh-huh. I mean, yes, sir."

"I hope so."

In the middle of the fifth round the captain suddenly blew a whistle. Dave, who was trying to find the range on Overby in the short time he'd have left to him before another punch sent him staggering away, suddenly fell back a couple of steps.

"You just fouled him, Overby," the lieutenant said

severely and untruthfully. "There'll be no fouls in this fight. I warned both of you that one foul blow would result in a draw being declared, and that's the way it's going to be. I rule that the fight has resulted in a draw."

Lawlor shook his head and tried to say that he hadn't been fouled. He must have managed to get at least a few words out; the captain looked quizzically at him.

"You're a brave man, Lawlor," he said. "Now I want you two to touch gloves as a sign that there's no more bad blood between you."

There was bad blood on Lawlor's part, though. He still wanted to kill that little son of a bitch Overby.

He came closer to the corporal, however, and held out both gloved hands. Overby hesitated and did the same thing. Four gloves touched.

In spite of his pained and dazed condition, Lawlor called out. There was some kind of a weight in each of the corporal's gloves, and when they rested against his own he was nearly knocked off his feet again.

He glared at Colbert, murder in his eyes.

The captain said quietly, "Any time you want trouble, Lawlor, the army is only too glad to oblige you from the lowest ranks upward."

Lawlor understood he was being told that Overby had been acting on orders. If he could have spoken clearly he'd have told everybody in the tent that he'd been triple-crossed, but the words wouldn't come. By the time he was able to say anything at all, the captain and Overby's second had taken off the loaded gloves and probably ditched the extra weights.

He did make up his mind to get hold of Overby on the following afternoon, drag him out to the boondocks, and beat the living crap out of him. By the time he got through with the corporal, not even Nina Field would be able to make any repairs in that weasel's face.

He waited till he saw Overby deep in conversation with Ken Hubbard. As he pounded over to the rock that Overby was sitting on, Dave couldn't help hearing what Overby said.

"Bravest man I ever saw," he was telling Ken Hubbard.

"He's all right, I guess," Hubbard drawled.

"He's a lot more than that. He must've known he couldn't win, but he kept on coming."

"I doubt if he knew anything except that he wanted to knock your head off."

"When you're in a fight, Sergeant, you get a pretty shrewd idea what your situation is. You might never say it to yourself, but you really know. Lawlor is a fellow with guts, believe me, guts and to spare. I don't know about you, but I'm damn glad Dave Lawlor is out here with us."

Lawlor stopped himself in midstride, teeth clenched. He couldn't fight the little bastard after that, and he knew it. The corporal had probably been ordered to praise hell out of Lawlor behind his back and to his face, all as a way of keeping the sergeant in line and preventing another blowup.

Goddammit, and damn the army, too, he told himself, and hurried away from the two men.

It was hard to stay sore at somebody who had nothing but praise for him, though, and in the next couple of days Lawlor and Overby got to be pretty good friends.

Four

NINA FIELD sat in her room at the United States Hospital in Saigon. Lamplight beat down on the desk, but Nina didn't care that the light was too strong. She was writing a letter, her pen moving with swift and determined strokes across unlined paper.

She was a dark-haired girl, well formed, with sharp, classic features. For a year and three-quarters she had been working at the hospital, and if she was in any way disappointed it was impossible to tell from her letters or the way she talked to the friends she had made in Saigon.

Nina was used to keeping thoughts to herself. As the youngest graduate in med school, for instance, she had thanked the dean courteously for his speech of commendation and had not let him or anybody else see that she was embarrassed at being pointed out for doing her work efficiently.

As a plastic surgeon, she'd found satisfaction in treating the scarred and the desperately unhappy people whose lives would be changed, they felt sure, if only their faces didn't have any blemish or their hands weren't shaped so badly. The trouble with their thinking was simply that such blemishes sometimes left scars on the mind, and a long time had to go past, a long time after the operation, before what might be called a "cure" could take place. But cures did happen, heaven knew, and that was a lot better for any patient than keeping the blemish.

If cases like those had accounted for most of her work in Cincinnati, she'd probably still have been there. For every salesman who felt he was losing out because he looked his age and wanted to be made to look younger, she was getting dozens of women who wanted their noses rounded off, their lips shaped a little differently, and other changes made for social reasons only. Every so often Nina felt that she ought to be working on the top floor of a beauty salon.

Every year she would go to visit her parents, who had retired and moved back to their home state, Georgia. On a visit some two years ago she had met a soldier-in-training at Fort Benning. David Lawlor was a handsome man with a devilish smile and merry eyes. He was a hard, competent man. They had dined together on their first date and a drunk had made some remarks about her. Nina had been willing to take it in stride, but Dave had stood up and gone over to that drunk's bar stool and put out a hand and sent that drunk clear across the room.

Later, when the drunk had been hauled out, she had said, "You did that very well."

"He was a nuisance and he had to be got rid of. Fighting is my trade, and I work pretty good at my trade. But I don't like to ram people any more than you like to operate on the sick. It's just something that's got to be done in both cases."

"And who decides you've got to ram somebody?"

"I do, or my boss. He's paying me, setting me up with a good salary and a pension. He's got reasons of his own for calling the tune, and I can't do a thing about it."

"Then you don't mind going to Vietnam."

"Vietnam is a job that somebody has to help get done, and I'm being trained for it."

"In other words, Dave, you're just a machine with no human feelings at all."

"What I am, Nina, is a man who has taken on a certain job and shouldn't complain if he gets it."

She had decided never to see Dave Lawlor again, but he wrote to her in a few days that he needed help from her. It seemed that the restaurant drunk had put in a complaint with army authorities, and Dave wanted her to speak up for him. She did, of course, and spent more

31

time with David Lawlor. As a result, the two of them had gone to bed together, and the vacation trip to Georgia had lasted much longer than she had expected.

It was surprising how trivial and foolish her job became when she got back to Cincinnati again. She was doing more useless cosmetic jobs than ever before, it seemed, and getting fed up. She hadn't become a surgeon for the same reason that other girls became beauticians. She wanted to use her skills in ways that would help her feel she was being of use to other people.

She resigned from the Cincinnati hospital staff without giving the real reason or hinting that she'd have any regrets in getting away from there. A long talk with Dave Lawlor and one or two others had helped Nina make up her mind about what to do next, and she took a staff appointment to the U.S. Hospital in Saigon.

Much more work came her way that could be called useful as well as important. The GI cases alone made her feel considerable satisfaction when they worked out well. Occasionally she had a Vietnamese soldier, and she was surprised and touched by the courtesy and gentleness of the men. She didn't see many Vietnamese, except on the operating table. Sometimes she'd go out with a staff doctor, and she spent Dave Lawlor's R and R time with him if she could get away too. Her life could be called insulated.

There was no keeping out the other cases, though, not even during wartime in this country. Some local bigwigs had to be kept reasonably happy, and their wives wanted face jobs as a sign of status. She was taking valuable time away from postoperative care on important cases in order to do a rash of operations on women who wanted to change the Oriental shape of their eyes—the sort of hack jobs that she had come out here to escape.

If Dave Lawlor was able to read between the lines of the letter she was writing to him, then he'd know that she wasn't feeling good about the job. But Dave Lawlor wasn't the kind of man who'd see anything unless it was pointed out to him; except, she supposed, the sight of an enemy soldier.

Four knocks sounded gently on the door as she was sealing the envelope.

"Open." The soft voice didn't belong to anybody who spoke English as his native tongue. "Please."

Nina stood and opened the door on a Vietnamese who was dressed like a hospital orderly. She didn't recognize him.

"Come with me," he said. "Please."

"Who are you, and what's wrong?"

She didn't see his right hand move, but a pistol appeared in it. "Come with me and ask no questions. Please. You will not be harmed."

Nina was surprised by her own coolness. She started out the door, but the intruder didn't step aside for her.

"Take emergency kit," he said. "Please."

"There'll be equipment near whichever room you—oh, all right."

The gun had been raised no more than half an inch or so, but she didn't need any stronger persuasion. She reached over to a chair for the emergency kit, which she knew would be filled. The man in the orderly's uniform walked back of her, indicating by only a softly spoken word or two that he wanted her to walk down the stairs and then outside. He always added "Please," and it always seemed like the afterthought it was.

She hadn't expected to be leaving the hospital grounds, and she supposed that the sight of an orderly back of her was sure to tip off any guard that something was wrong.

They didn't seem to have interrupted their progress, as far as Nina could tell, but the man had somehow found a way to shuck the uniform by the time she got close to the guard in the sandbagged metal bunker. The guard gestured for both of them to leave.

There was a car on the corner, with another Vietnamese back of the wheel. Nina stepped into the back, at the orderly's command-followed-by-request.

The orderly—she would always think of him as that—glanced at Nina as she settled down in the back seat of the old car. Then he touched the driver's arm and came around in back to sit near her. As soon as he closed the door the car started.

She glanced out the window at the October night, but the orderly spoke sharply to her, and she turned to face him.

"Look down," he said, probably repeating himself. "Look at your lap or the floor, if you wish, but not outside."

"You forgot to say 'Please,'" she told him, if only to see him get rattled.

He added coolly, "Please."

Nina looked down at the blue knee-length dress she was wearing. She could smell rubber in the car and cold fish past the window. It didn't seem possible to be anywhere in Saigon except a surgical theater and not smell cold fish. She didn't believe that there had been a rise in her blood pressure from the minute she had seen the gun.

"You may get out now," the orderly said a few minutes later when the car stopped. "Please."

She did, and saw that she was on a long, narrow street with two-story houses and not a store in sight.

"Enter the fourth house that you come to."

She tightened the grip on her black bag as she opened the door the orderly had indicated. This was a big and well-furnished room with drapes, soft chairs, twin sofas, a cocktail table, and reproductions on the walls.

"Next room. Please."

The hallway led to another room in which there was a huge bed almost in the exact center. For the first time since the gun had been pulled on her, Nina drew back.

"You mustn't be alarmed," a new voice said.

The man had probably been walking the room; he had apparently turned around when he reached the farthest wall. He wasn't much past twenty years old, and he was tall for a Vietnamese. His upper lip was a shade lighter

34

than the skin on the balance of his face, which probably meant that he had shaved off a mustache not long ago. He spoke English carefully, but with a trace of accent.

Nina asked, "Will you tell me why I've been brought here?"

"Of course." The man looked surprised. "I have to, if you're going to do the service I want."

"There is no reason why you should need my professional services."

"There is one reason."

"Am I to be told what it is by the time the war is over?"

His eyes glinted appreciatively. "I am wanted by the police. My face is known, and I cannot escape Saigon unless an operation is performed and my face is changed. Do I make myself clear?"

"Perfectly. There are limits, though, to what I can do if I agree to help."

"For instance?"

"If I have to do the operation here, I'll be working without much necessary equipment."

"You can do what has to be done, I'm sure." He glanced at the black bag.

"I can't guarantee freedom from pain for a while. Perhaps for quite a while."

"In the facial area, do you mean?"

"Not entirely. I have to decide on an acceptable donor section from which to remove skin for a graft. I will take some skin from another part of your body and make sure that it retains a blood supply in transit. In that way the newly grafted skin won't look like a dead area. But there'll be more pain than you'd have if you were operated on under ideal conditions."

"I am not a child. I can withstand pain." He frowned. "Does the skin from the donor section, as you call it, grow back? I mean, the section where the graft was taken from. It will not always be a hole, so to speak. Or will it?"

"I only graft two layers of skin; otherwise the skin would be reduced in thickness. And I'll have included only part of the corium with the epithelium." She smiled lightly. "The skin grows back, of course, but it can be a difficult process."

"I accept that fact."

"I can't guarantee a successful operation, either," she pointed out. "The best chances of success come with what we call a partial-thickness graft. When you work with facial areas, though, a PT graft can't be used. You might be scarred or wounded for life, and all through no fault of my own."

"So." He stood with arms akimbo. "If it should go badly with me, you can expect to hear from my friends."

"It might go badly with you no matter how hard I try to do a good job. You might even lose your life."

He shrugged. "There is no choice but to go through with it."

"You must be wanted for much more than a trivial offense if you're willing to risk your life on an operation like this one."

"Quite true."

"Murder?"

"In my unhappy country nowadays, the murder of one individual is unimportant, unless the person has a large place in the country's affairs."

"You murdered an official, then. I take it, then, that you're a member of the National Liberation Front."

"I am, yes." He sized her up through heavy-lidded eyes. "I tell you this for the reason that it may help you to realize my friends can revenge themselves upon you if the work does not come out the way I wish. Or if you should refuse to help."

"I see."

"Now that I come to think of it, you have indeed given me an idea. Your attitude has."

He raised his voice and spoke to the orderly in Vietnamese. Nina would have given a considerable amount of money to know what he was saying, but she decided against putting the question to him when he was finished.

36

"You stay—and ask no questions," he replied. "There are other doctors to care for your patients."

She was led upstairs to a dingy room that held a cot and had two crude framed paintings on the walls. Light came from a bare bulb suspended from the ceiling. The notion of staying in this place for the best part of three days made her want to shudder, and she barely managed to control herself.

"How will I call you in case of need?"

"My name is Ban. You call. I will hear." He left the room, pausing only to bow very briefly from the waist. Nina heard a key in the lock.

She inspected her surroundings. It was possible to climb out the window, but there wasn't anything like a fire-escape route and she'd have to jump two stories to the narrow residential street. She could very easily be killed. The door wouldn't give way under the pressure she could apply, and there wasn't a chance of getting at the lock. Just because some things in South Vietnam were done differently from the way they might be handled at home didn't mean that they weren't being done sensibly, according to local lights. The lock in this door, for instance, was noisy and awkward, but she wouldn't be able to unlock it and the darn thing would probably last forever.

Nina waited till the orderly had been able to settle down to some other chore and then shouted his name a couple of times. There was a pause, and then his steps sounded on the stairs and he unlocked the door.

"I must clean my instruments or they'll become rusty and not be of any use to me during the next three days," she said.

He went back with her to the operating room, rather than leave her alone so she'd have a chance to climb out the window.

Nina had to make a production out of putting the instruments under soap and water and then packing them inside the black bag. The orderly glared at her for taking him away from whatever chore had been keeping him busy a few minutes ago.

The patient suddenly moaned.

Nina would have ignored the postanesthesia response, but the orderly wheeled around on her. She walked over to the bed and satisfied herself about the nature of the momentary difficulty. The orderly looked worried.

That was when she decided on taking a chance. She said, "I think I may have to do the bandaging all over again."

As she had expected, the orderly began to look pale.

"Once more?" he asked weakly.

"I have been called to do the best for my patient that I possibly can." Nina made her voice sound cool. "If you can't stand the sight of skin and blood and discoloration, I would suggest that you leave."

He started to shake his head, but the idea made him flinch.

"You look as if you're going to vomit, and if I'm working on the patient I don't want any distractions. Please leave now, and do it before I work on your friend."

She knew she held the cards. The orderly had enough strength to glare at her, but he opened the door, closed it, and leaned heavily against it.

Nina decided against taking the black bag with her. She ran on tiptoes to the French window, got it open, and managed to sit on the outer sill. From there it was a ten-foot jump to the ground. She made it and started to run down the street. At the corner she turned right and found herself on a wider street, a shopping section where the smell of fish was almost overpowering. A taxi was racketing down the street. Nina signaled with both hands waving. The driver nodded and stopped his cab twenty feet away from her. Nina ran to it.

Mr. Rupert Honeybone didn't much enjoy working at night, but then there wasn't much in the Saigon assignment that he did enjoy. Mr. Honeybone was a bureaucrat. He knew how to convince the people over him that he was working harder than he actually was, and he had a shrewdly developed knack for making his job seem like the most important one at the embassy. When he genuinely had to work hard, Mr. Honeybone knew how to take risks and shortcuts that would cost him the job if he were ever caught at it.

Mr. Honeybone was a State Department specialist in Asian affairs, and he had gone through tours of duty in Sukarno's Indonesia, as well as in Thailand and Hong Kong. He could pick up a new language as quickly as some other fellow might get a working knowledge of golf. The people who didn't like him would sometimes call him a cookie pusher, whatever that meant. Sometimes, when he was at a party and feeling as if he might get a glow on, he would call himself a political grease monkey.

Night work bothered him, though. For one thing, the notion of putting in any hours but nine to five was enough to make him shudder. Second, night was the time for crank calls and callers. He didn't know why, but he had never worked in an embassy where the screwballs didn't wait till sundown and then come down on the embassy skeleton staff in droves. When the full moon was out, the cranks would practically stampede each other in their eagerness to get the attention of a staff member.

It didn't surprise him too much, then, that the night secretary came in and said that there was a young woman outside and that she had a strange story he ought to hear. She was an employee at the U.S. Hospital, Pettis added, a doctor.

Mr. Honeybone's well-shaped brows darted up to a point near his hairline. He had the bureaucrat's deep-rooted distrust of an educated woman, and he wasn't looking forward to the interview.

The girl turned out to be attractive in a dark, high-cheekboned way. Her clothes were rumpled. Even though she was trying to be calm, there was a frightened look deep in her eyes.

"What can I do for you, Miss—uh . . . ?"

41

"I'm Doctor Field. I work at the U.S. Hospital."

"It's a formality, doctor, but of course you can prove what you say."

"I don't have any proof with me. My purse—my emergency bag . . ."

Probably she was a hanger-on at some civilian firm or other. Mr. Honeybone made a point of looking at his watch, then lifted a paper from his In tray and kept it in front of him.

"Oh?" Mr. Honeybone actually did look at the paper, now. It was a request for added supplies needed to run the embassy, which would probably have to be pried out of the U.S. Operations Mission with a couple of crowbars and an ax handle. USOM was pretty good about some things, but when it came to . . .

The girl was already launched on her story, which sounded as wild as Mr. Honeybone would have expected from a girl who carried no identification. She had been kidnapped, it seemed, and forced to perform an operation on someone. Operation! Now *there* was a brand-new word for it.

"When they find out I escaped they'll come for me," she said. "And I know that the patient was a Vietcong worker. He admitted it. He practically said he had killed an important man and wanted to get away and that the police were watching for him."

Mr. Honeybone sighed. The girl must have read about the recent killing of Ho Bin Giap and put two and two together in building up a tissue of lies. Some of these cranks were amazingly creative.

The girl stopped herself and asked calmly, "Do you think I'm making up all this?"

"No, of course not."

"Is there any way I can prove the story to your satisfaction?"

"I accept the truth of it, of course," Mr. Honeybone said, lying smoothly. "A few details might help, though. For instance, can you tell me which street you were taken to?"

42

"No, I can't. I was ordered to sit so that I wouldn't be able to look out the window, and when I ran away I was in too much of a hurry to see where I was."

"Can you describe the street?"

"It was narrow, with a lot of houses on it."

"How far is it from the embassy?"

"Forty minutes by taxi."

Any number of streets could have fitted the description, such as it was.

"Can you describe the man you say you operated on?"

She could and did. The description could have fitted the wanted man, On Ne Clo, and any number of others as well.

Mr. Honeybone sat back and allowed himself to wonder how much of the story he might be able to prove. If the girl was who she said, there had to be some records. The first job was to get hold of them.

"If you'll pardon me, Doctor," he said, "I'll be back in a few minutes."

In Pettis's office, which was smaller and bulging with papers that had to be processed showing in plain sight— Mr. Honeybone always kept his Out tray filled, his In tray half-filled, and the balance of the In papers at one side of a lower desk drawer—he put through a call to the U.S. Hospital.

The night receptionist's description of Dr. Field checked with the girl in his office, but he took down some statistics about the doctor's previous affiliations and decided to see if the girl's story would confirm them.

"And by the way, Pettis, you'd best come in with me," Mr. Honeybone told the secretary. "If I have to ease her out, I want to do it quickly, and I'll need help."

Pettis asked, "One of the bugaboos?"

"I'd almost swear to it." Mr. Honeybone smiled bleakly. "In fact, Pettis, I'd stake your life on it. That's how strongly I feel."

The girl's answers matched his information, though, and Mr. Honeybone was willing to agree that she was Dr.

43

Nina Field; but it didn't follow that Dr. Field hadn't started imagining things.

"I suppose we'll have to put a bodyguard on you, in the circumstances," he said, resigned to the inevitable by now. "I want to thank you for coming in so quickly with the information."

"It seems to me that those men will try to get away, but you shouldn't have a hard time finding them if some policemen go to one of those streets that fits the description I gave you."

"Yes, yes," Mr. Honeybone said hurriedly. "Thanks very much, Doctor."

"Don't forget that the patient will be all bandaged up."

"But according to you, Doctor Field, the patient only has to be hidden for seventy-two hours, and then he'll have a new face, which you gave him. Under those circumstances, a search would be useless."

She shuddered. "I took grafts, but I didn't do anything with them. I only pretended to. The change I made in his face was to scar him."

"Excuse me?"

"I carved the letters VC on each of his cheeks," Nina Field said quietly. "He can't hide them or get them off."

Mr. Honeybone sat for a second's stunned silence. He could certainly imagine the hard-to-find On Ne Clo with the letters on both cheeks that told everybody in the world that he was part of the Cong. It was worth assuming that she was telling the strict truth.

"If this is correct, Doctor, you won't need a bodyguard after all," he said, and turned to Pettis. "See to the police dragnet, will you?"

"Yes, sir," Pettis said. He'd heard a condensed version of the whole story from Mr. Honeybone back in his own cluttered office a few minutes ago, and he knew what instructions to give. He rushed out on the way to his own office again.

"Well, Doctor Field, you've probably done an important piece of work for us all under difficult conditions,"

44

Mr. Honeybone said. "It wouldn't surprise me if you received some kind of award."

That was when Mr. Honeybone got the biggest surprise of the night. He had expected a crank, but found out that she was a person of some standing who had been very helpful; and now that she must have realized her story had been accepted as the truth, she lost her temper. Dr. Nina Field suddenly clenched her fists and leaned forward angrily.

"Award!" Her eyes blazed. "Do you realize that I've spent my whole life trying to fix people, trying to help people? Now for the first time I've had to destroy a human face, the first time in my career—and you have the gall to say that I can expect an award for it."

Mr. Honeybone sat back, surprised by an outburst that he sensed would be very rare with such a self-contained woman. If he hadn't already put matters underway, he'd have called everything back. It would look bad for anybody in his position, though, to let others think he couldn't make up his mind. The girl had saved her loss of temper until she knew that he believed her. But she certainly didn't mind acting like a crank.

Five

TAM HUNG was the biggest of three hamlets, and the name was generally applied to the smaller ones that clustered around it like barnacles. Tam Hung itself was made up of a line of thatched huts along with some wooden houses that had been repaired with patches of tin roofing. There was one whitewashed concrete building, and the red-yellow flag of the Republic of South Vietnam flew from the pole on top of it.

Hardly a man could be seen among the six hundred families who made up the Tam Hung complex. All the young men were in the army on one side or another, and a few had deserted. There were women with babies, and old men who couldn't take care of themselves too well any longer.

Nobody knew why the people wanted to stay in Tam Hung instead of going to Saigon, say, and finding relative security in the capital. Tam Hung was situated in a place where Vietcong raids took place practically every other day. The Cong would tax every farmer ten percent of his rice yield, and if there was a young man in town they were more likely than not to take him away for their army. The South Vietnamese government would take away taxes, too, so that the people of Tam Hung were paying two separate sets of taxes and not getting the slightest protection for the outlay.

It was the Americans who finally offered protection, but at the cost of the farmers giving up their land entirely while the war lasted. The South Vietnamese government had built a camp very near the town, and when the Americans came everything suddenly changed. There weren't more than twelve Americans, but they talked the language and tried to be friendly. They set up health programs for a start, and did other things.

The price of American protection soon became clear. They hemmed in Tam Hung with barbed wire, and nobody could get in or out unless he had some kind of a paper to show a soldier at a certain point. And then the Americans took families away from their farms because there was danger to them from the Vietcong and set them down in the village, where they didn't have anything to do.

Only, of course, there were some people who would sneak out at night and go up to the fields they had left. For instance, Ha Binh, who wanted to see her husband again. . . .

Nguyen Van Mieng stood stiffly in the middle of the wide field. Sunlight hammered down on his thin face and glinted off his steel-gray sideburns.

"Land," he said, looking ahead of him. "Always I want land under me."

"You could be killed for coming back here," Ha Binh said. A small woman with a long nose and warm brown eyes, she purposely kept her voice on the one emotionless level.

Her husband put out strong, wiry fingers to circle her right arm. "I could be killed for staying in the army, too," he said roughly, his own lips a bloodless line. "A man is nothing without his land, his house, his ancestral tombs, his place in the world clear to him because it's at his sides or under his feet."

Ha Binh looked around at dirt and clumps of grass embedded with dust that made the nostrils twitch.

"We must begin, then," she said.

He nodded. The pigs had been killed or taken away by the Vietcong. Two water buffalo had been left behind, but they were so scrawny that it was impossible to get work out of them. Finding food for the water buffalo took the best part of their first afternoon. Nguyen Van

47

Mieng put on the rice farmer's traditional black pajamas, a uniform the Vietcong had taken over along with so many other things, and he did what had to be done first of all.

He had hoped that the family house with its three altars would still be standing, but it had been destroyed by cannon fire from one side or both. He and his wife had to sleep in a hole in the ground for that night at least, and their sleep was troubled by the sound of gunfire.

Nguyen Van Mieng was used to hard work, so it didn't bother him too much. He tilled and softened the ground and learned by his own mistakes and went to sleep at night and went out every morning with his own land under his feet. He had never been well fed, and now he was getting scrawny. Thick lines in a semicircle from nostrils to points just above the chin became thicker in his sun-darkened face.

Ha Binh helped him as much as she could. More often than not, though, she had her own work cut out for her in getting food for a meal. They were lucky to be having a couple of meals every day, and sometimes Ha Binh would manage to get cold fish for herself and her husband.

Ha Binh's nerves were getting thin, too. She'd make lists in her mind of the sort of clothes she'd like to have, and she could never sleep past three o'clock. She would start pacing the earth by that time. The sound of her footsteps always reached Nguyen Van Mieng, who didn't complain but lay back with cupped hands behind his back and waited until he could watch sunrise coming over the land that his father and grandfather and great grandfather had owned.

One night Ha Binh set herself to warm the fish in some sort of utensil she had made out of bits and pieces left from the house. The food was good enough to bring warm spit up along the tongue.

Not till he was finished did he say to her, "Let us hope that the smoke was not observed."

Ha Binh looked worried. "By the Cong?"

"I hope not."

But the hope was useless. A tall, thin Vietcong in black pajamas showed up on the next morning. He scuffed the land with the toes of his sandals as if he owned it himself, and searched their belongings in case there was anything valuable that they might be keeping. There wasn't. He sneered at Nguyen Van Mieng and Ha Binh, then told them that they would have to pay the VC tax of ten percent of the rice crop and that they had better not have anything to do with the Americans or they would both be killed.

Nguyen Van Mieng nodded, but Ha Binh's hands stole toward her husband's in worry that she didn't bother to hide.

The work went on. Nguyen Van Mieng put a wheelbarrow together. He practically built the ox cart all over again and used water buffalo to move it. With the help of the water buffalo, now a little heavier and better able to work, he and his wife were starting to feel hopeful about their situation for the first time. One afternoon, though, the man from the Vietcong came back and took the healthier water buffalo for himself.

"Our need is greater than yours," he said, patting his stomach, which looked pretty big to Ha Binh's angry eyes.

Nguyen Van Mieng sat quietly on the ground, muscles moving in his chin. His sweaty-red face had become white in the last few minutes. He couldn't meet her eyes, but stared up at the place where the house had been, the house with its big black bed and three Buddhist altars and its shelter for the pigs.

They kept working. Ha Binh had got hold of a pair of coolie hats, which were their only shield from the sun. Ha Binh had always talked nineteen to the dozen and bubbled over with plans for the next days or weeks or months, but now she moved around their fields with a firm set to her lips. Her face had become blood-red, and her hands seemed to have shrunk so that anything she touched made a dry sound like old paper. She had started to bite her fingernails, too, since coming back here.

"How long are we going to stay?" she demanded of him one evening. Her semicircular gesture with the hands included the shelter and the fields.

"This is my home," he said. "And yours."

"Which of the soldiers is going to kill us?"

"If you want to leave, do so."

"I stay with my husband."

Nguyen Van Mieng nodded, then eased the sandals off his feet and dropped them to earth, wriggling his toes as he said a long, drawn-out "Ah-hhh!"

If he hadn't been taking it easy, he might've been able to find some hiding-place when the helicopter came over on patrol. As it was he stayed in one place, frozen, as if he hoped he wouldn't be seen by the sharp-eyed American pilot.

When the helicopter was gone, she said to him, "For one moment you relax, and then the trouble comes. They will come back and take you, and then the Vietcong will come, too. Between one side and the other, what will become of us?"

"Somehow this will work out."

"You're a deserter," she said. "You'll be shot by the Americans or the Cong."

"If I die, it will happen here at my home."

Ha Binh walked up and down that night, her teeth biting down on a forefinger. When she put both hands behind her back after a while, there was a hard set to her thin lips.

She was trying to sleep, her face in the crook of one arm, when the Americans got there. A thin and tall young one was in command of the other man, who drove what Ha Binh thought of as the machine cart. The other fellow looked stupid, but his eyes roamed the field in searching for traps.

Nguyen Van Mieng waited for the tall, thin one to come up to where he was. The sight of his fields generally made his heart beat a little more noisily in his ears, but now he only looked at one corner of his fields at a time.

50

His hard sunburned fingers moved in and out, in and out. . . .

"You have put your life in danger," the thin American said, scratching his chin with a blunt thumbnail. "The Vietcong are dangerous men."

Nguyen Van Mieng nodded. "I know. I was fighting on the same side as your people."

"Did you leave without permission?"

"I wanted to be back on my land."

"You know how important it is to stay and see that the Cong is beaten. You know—"

The second man suddenly called out something and ran to a point back of a tree. The thin American whirled around, and his breath caught. The shelter wasn't far from them, and he ran with Ha Binh, shielding her from bullets. He pushed her down against the earth where she might be safe.

Bullets had sounded, many of them clack-clacking around their heads. Ha Binh looked for her man.

The American said to her, "I'll get him."

He went into a crouch and started running toward where Nguyen Van Mieng had stood. Her husband, too, was running for the shelter. The American fired in the general direction of the tree behind which the VC was hiding. The death threat would distract that VC, he hoped, from doing any harm to Nguyen Van Mieng.

The American suddenly stared down at his gun and cursed, then let it fall to the earth. Even Ha Binh understood that the gun had no more bullets in it.

A Vietcong in black pajamas appeared from back of a banana tree. He carried a large gun and raised it to fire.

Ha Binh saw what happened next but couldn't call out. Nguyen Van Mieng's path had accidentally taken him to a point directly in front of the American. He tried to scuttle out of the way but couldn't do it. The VC fired three times. Nguyen Van Mieng's body stiffened, and he fell lengthwise. Ha Binh knew without having to think about it that her man was dead.

51

At almost the same second, the Vietcong's bullets had been fired so quickly, the other American soldier, the one who she had thought looked so stupid, fired twice. The Vietcong crumpled almost like her man's house had done under the impact of weapons.

There was a stunned quiet. Ha Binh cradled her head in her arms and rocked back and forth. Gently a man's arms shook her shoulders.

"We're taking you away from here," the thin American said.

Ha Binh surprised herself. She had wanted nothing better than to go away with her husband, but now he was dead and she didn't want his land to be left alone once more.

"No," she said. "No. I will stay."

"The Vietcong will come back in force and kill you and perhaps do worse to you before they kill."

"I will stay."

The American made no further request. She felt herself being lifted and made to walk toward the mechanical cart in which he and the other had come.

"I will be back," she called out. "If you force me to go, I will be back."

The American didn't say anything to that.

When Ken Hubbard and Corporal Overby got back to Tam Hung, Ken made a point of introducing Ha Binh to a woman her own age, a woman with a husband in the army and three kids to raise. Ken figured that the widow, Ha Binh, would have her work cut out helping the other woman.

As it turned out, Ken had underestimated Ha Binh. She brought in another woman to help the first one and spent her own time trying to get away. The guards had been tipped off about her, though, and no excuse could get her out of the barbed-wire compound and back to the field where death waited for her.

Ha Binh would sit with hands in front of her and

52

stare at nothing for day after day. She was getting thinner, and when she talked it was as if she had to bring the words up from a long distance and over a road that hadn't been used before.

Ken took the whole problem to Captain Colbert. Matt Colbert saw that Ken was bothered about it and gave the matter more consideration than he might have otherwise.

"You're not out to marry this girl, I take it."

"'Course not, sir," Ken said in his soft Ozark drawl.

"We might be able to do something for her up here," Colbert said. "There's a kitchen, after all, and I would think she might be some help to the counterpart chef."

"That's a fine idea, sir," Ken Hubbard said heartily. "Her man took some bullets meant for me, and I sure owe her something. I appreciate this, Captain."

"Let's hope the girl will," Colbert said dryly. "That'll be all, Sergeant."

Ken brought Ha Binh to the camp, and she was put to work in the kitchen. She did enough small jobs to free at least one Viet soldier for fieldwork. She didn't complain but walked around with glazed eyes and lips trembling as if the slightest trouble would make her cry.

Ken made a habit of looking in on her at least once a day. Hardly a word passed between them. Every so often they would simply look at each other and make no real response.

Ken missed one day at the camp. He was a demolitions man, and he'd gone upcountry to blast away some trees in getting ready for an expected set-to with Charlie. The idea behind it was to ambush Charlie at a certain area, and when Charlie hopped into a nearby ditch for cover he'd find that the ditch had been mined. If things went right, Charlie wouldn't know anything more in this world.

Ken and Overby were stranded by rain, though, and had to stay overnight, sleeping on ponchos and taking turns at watch. When he looked in on Ha Binh next afternoon her eyes lighted as soon as she saw him.

"Is everything well, Ha Binh?" he asked softly.

She didn't answer that but instead asked him, "And with you?"

"Very well."

She looked down, the way a modest Asian woman is supposed to do when in the presence of a man. Ken murmured something or other and left.

When Matt Colbert asked about the situation with the girl he had taken in, Ken was able to give an encouraging report. "So far, so good, Captain," he said. "At least, she's not just a few steps from suicide, the way she had been. In fact, I think she's getting some pride back."

"Fine," Colbert said, then shuffled papers on his desk and changed the subject. "Now about the Duc Trang ambush . . ."

Outside the headquarters building, some native shouted. Ken and Colbert wheeled toward the door of the orderly room, and Colbert picked up an M-16 rifle as he ran.

The trouble had happened around the corner, near the kitchen area. A Vietnamese soldier was standing doubled up. Ha Binh glowered at him, a sharp kitchen knife raised in one hand.

Matt's Vietnamese counterpart, Captain Dac Hee Quang, came running up from his quarters. He was a small man and seemed out of breath.

Ken asked quietly, "What happened, Ha Binh?"

She turned to him and started talking much more promptly than she'd have done with anybody else. "This one came to me and said I must make love with him or he would have me sent away from camp and into the fields where the Cong would find me."

"And you acted like an angry woman might be expected to, in some ways." He nodded. "I'm glad you cared enough not to let him have his way."

"I wanted to frighten him."

Dac Hee Quang drew a deep breath. It looked to Ken as if the Vietnamese captain was suffering sympathetic pains with the soldier. Dac Hee Quang had certainly

54

pulled both hands down till they rested tightly together near his crotch.

"The woman must go."

Ken saw Matt Colbert nod slowly. "Very well, Captain," Colbert said. "There shall be no difficulty between us over this matter."

Ken took her back to the village and asked one of the older women to look after her in case there was any trouble. The woman agreed after Ken gave her a few piaster notes for her trouble. He went back to his usual job of blowing up certain areas and setting traps, earning his hazard pay of fifty dollars extra every month.

Before leaving Ha Binh he told her that he wouldn't be able to look in on her every day. He had last seen her on Monday, and it was Friday before he went into the village again. The change in her appearance shocked him. Her face was almost as red as a beet, and her eyes watered all the time. She lay on a straw pallet in the same room with the bed that the old woman used. He won a smile and a nod from her, but she didn't say much. It was hard to keep from noticing that an egg in its shell had been tied to her wrist with rope, but he was so upset that he couldn't bring himself to ask her about it.

He found the crone who was supposed to look after Ha Binh. She was in front of the hut cleaning eels.

"You haven't been helping Ha Binh."

"Certainly I have," the crone snapped. "Didn't I call in the provincial chief when I saw that she wasn't well? Of course I did. Who else would have tied the egg to her hand?"

"The egg?" He stared. "It's supposed to cure something, I suppose."

"If anything can cure her," the crone said darkly. "She suffers from the winter sickness."

Ken, who hadn't been cross-trained as a medic, realized that he ought to have guessed that Ha Binh was seriously ill. He used a field phone in his truck and called the base for Sid Wheeler, one of the medics, to come around.

Wheeler showed up in less than twenty minutes. He was a tall, quick-moving Negro who did the work of two people and never complained except when there wasn't any work for him to do.

His first examination of Ha Binh took only a little while. Ken, pacing outside the hut, could hear Wheeler fumbling with his medical bag and murmuring soothingly to Ha Binh. Ken supposed that the girl was scared of a medical examination because she'd never had one.

Wheeler was shaking his head when he came out of the hut.

"It's pneumonia," he said. "Maybe she'll make it, Ken, but I can't swear one way or the other. I shot her full of penicillin and told the woman who lives here with her to keep her warm at all times, and gave her some p-notes."

"Thanks, Sid. I'll look in every day."

"You'll probably see me here." Wheeler grinned. "One thing, though. The girl wouldn't let me near her till I said that you'd sent me. Then it was all right."

In spite of everything, Ken smiled.

"Are you hot for the chick?" Wheeler asked with cheerful ruthlessness. "If you are, it's going to take a little time before you can gung-ho with her."

"I haven't thought about it," Ken drawled.

"Okay, okay, you look like you want to cut me up with little knives," Wheeler complained. "Oh, by the way, Ken, you noticed the egg on her wrist, I suppose. I didn't disturb it. You leave it alone too."

"If she believes in it, okay."

"Of course she believes in it," Wheeler said with wide-eyed innocence that couldn't have fooled a baby. "You know that albumen does wonders for pneumonia."

Ken very nearly laughed.

It took two weeks of constant care on the crone's part, along with Wheeler's visits every day, before it seemed that Ha Binh might be turning the corner back to health. Ken was dropping by as often as he could, so he didn't notice the changes as her color improved and she was able to eat more and more normally. He had the impression that his visits were the high spot of her day, and he wished he could have brought magazines to distract her or stayed longer on each visit.

Ha Binh needed two more weeks of bed rest before she was able to walk around, and by that time Ken realized he'd become strongly attracted to her. They talked together and it seemed that Ha Binh's life was very much like what he had known in the Kentucky hills, a hard life in which you tried to make the stubborn land yield food and, indirectly, clothing and shelter. She had a sense of humor, too, in a quiet and indirect Asian way, and all in all was the most feminine creature he had ever known.

Ken started to say so while they were talking one afternoon and then stopped himself. Ha Binh cocked her head inquiringly but didn't ask what he'd been about to say.

"You're . . . uh, nice," Ken said finally. "Maybe we can talk about us—I mean, talk about *things*, some other time."

He started to get up, minutes before he was supposed to meet Dave Lawlor in the concrete building.

Ha Binh said nothing.

He added, "Tomorrow, I'll tell you something that's been on my mind. Yes, that's right, Ha Binh, tomorrow."

And he got away from there, realizing that he had been on the point of suggesting that he and Ha Binh get married.

He hurried over to the concrete building and had to wait twenty minutes for Lawlor to join him.

Ken didn't show up on the next day or the day after that. The Battle of Duc Trang had got underway.

PART TWO

Six

Duc Trang didn't have any more genuine relation to the Tam Hung complex than a callus to a foot. It was separated from Tam Hung by a swatch of jungle, and the Vietcong had been using that area to launch attacks on the base and sometimes on the village itself.

Over the last few weeks, Ken Hubbard and two Viet counterparts had taken the lead in mining the section. Charlie would generally use it at night and keep to open patches of ground. Ken and his counterparts, sometimes helped by Corporal Overby, would generally dig ditches that looked like natural areas of shelter, and then mine them. Charlie soon started digging his own ditches, though, and the traps didn't work well any more. As long as Charlie could still use the Duc Trang section, he was ahead of the game.

In order to destroy him, a search-and-destroy operation had to be set up. Matt Colbert managed to persuade his Viet counterpart that the mission would be successful. Dac Hee Quang finally gave his okay to go ahead with it. Maybe it was a coincidence that on the day the operation was supposed to start he managed to leave the base for what he claimed was important government business at Qhi Nhon.

Bombers had been working the jungle for some hours before Matt Colbert's men and a company of Vietnamese were scheduled to go in. The sky was lighted up with bomb bursts and occasional fires. One of the bombardiers, a fellow named Harry Chiffinch, got caught in an open bomb-bay door and hung by his arms till the pilot could swing around over a body of water. Then he dropped. He was seen to swim out of the water and to wave and gesture to somebody else in a friendly way. The other soldier was seen by flare light to be a Vietcong who didn't live long after letting Harry Chiffinch fool him at night. As for Chiffinch himself, he might very well have lived to tell the tale, but one of the mined ditches finished him—he was blown to pieces.

Colbert's men and the Viets went in at exactly eighteen hundred hours, and the jungle soon smelled of woodsmoke, gunpowder, and death.

As they parachuted in, they realized that Charlie had managed to hide a mortar crew and that the mortars were now throwing white-phosphorous shells. When Charlie could get close enough, he was pitching claymore mines.

A number of Hueys showed up to drop eighty-one-millimeter shells on places that Jerry Garfine calmly pointed out by radio contact with the B team. The mortar crew probably shifted positions in advance, and the battery survived as an effective unit. Chinook copters dropped 105-millimeter howitzers that had been sling-loaded over their twin-turbine engines. The mortar was still, but nobody knew whether it had been knocked out of action.

Just when Charlie was doing better than before, Ken Hubbard noticed a small silver chopper practically staggering around overhead and knew it was the one that belonged to Colonel Esterbrook, who used it to prowl around over battles to see how his men were making out.

Some of them were doing all right.

Sid Wheeler, not having any medic work on hand, managed to get hold of a Czech burp gun from a dead Charlie and tried to turn it on some other men. It wasn't much good, though, and Wheeler had to duck into the brush and scoot out of there.

Dave Lawlor's M-16 became overheated at one point in the battle, and he cursed a blue streak and started throwing grenades. The pineapples were effective, but the Viets, seeing that his gun wasn't working, pulled back.

Lawlor cursed in English, in Bru, and in a native dialect that he had picked up on Okinawa at the SF base, but the men cowered and wouldn't move.

He stood up, as good as in the teeth of crossfire, and gestured to the men back of him.

"Are you men or are you rabbits? Come on the hell with me."

But when he started out he was alone—and in less than a minute he was feeling damn sorry for those Viets. Charlie had lobbed one of his white-phosphorous beauties straight at the ditch where the men had been crouched and quaking. There was a flash of light, and then everybody in the ditch was quiet except for the ones who moaned.

Lawlor ducked for cover back of a banyan tree and tried to figure out his next move. He decided he'd be better off with another Viet team so that at least he would get some chance to fight.

As he started to run back, he saw a number of Cong approach quietly, guided by the sound of moaning. They reached for the wounded, as Lawlor could make out by occasional flare light, and started propping them against another banyan some twenty-five feet away. Lawlor held his fire, wondering what these Charlies were up to and whether they were planning to save the lives of a number of South Vietnamese soldiers.

He didn't have to wait long before finding out what the Charlies were up to. A pair of them stationed themselves in front the other tree and started pumping bullets into the wounded. Lawlor knew he'd better do nothing if he wanted a chance to get out of this in one piece, so he had to listen to some of the moans turn into shrieks and then get cut off very quickly.

One moan could still be heard, and a Charlie bayoneted that man. The moan grew more faint but didn't stop. The Vietcong raised his bayonet and cut that man from the top of the head to the crotch. When he was finished the wounded man didn't make any more sounds.

The VC stepped back, satisfied at last—and then Lawlor risked his own life by shooting that Charlie neatly through the head. He ran away in a hail of bullets, thanking his lucky stars that Charlie's guns were such cheap junk. With anything like good sights Lawlor would've had his head handed to him, and he knew it.

Matt Colbert always wanted to be with his men, but the Viet lieutenant acting as his counterpart was simply too reckless and could've killed both of them. Lieutenant Hec Ma Drang would stand in a clearing and scream at the enemy, shaking his fists and throwing rocks. If Colbert had put a gun into his hands, Drang would simply have thrown it. He was tall for a Vietnamese and, like the ruling members of his government, he hailed from North Vietnam but had left in a hurry when the Ho regime took control.

Drang paced the jungle path, hands behind his back. Matt, fuming because he couldn't lose his temper with the man, held an M-16 in one hand and hit his thigh with the other.

Drang finally asked, "Why do you keep me here instead of with my men?"

"For your own good and mine," Matt said carefully. "We can get a clearer picture of the fighting and not be so emotionally involved. We both worry too much about the men."

"Ah." Lieutenant Drang's vanity was tickled. He smiled and stiffened. "In my case, it is more complex. I am a fighter and I can't bear not to be fighting."

Matt kept from saying that the lieutenant was a shouter instead of being a fighter.

"All the same," Drang added, "I'd like very much to be in the thick of it."

"I guess we'll have to move up," Matt agreed slowly, "but we'd better do it without giving away our position."

"Of course, Captain. That goes without saying."

Matt tried not to feel discouraged as he took the first steps closer to the heart of the action. He couldn't see what his men were doing and had to hope that their good training would pay off once more. But what use is training when one of your own men accidentally fires on you or a grenade falls short?

He was saved from taking the lieutenant any farther just then, because Drang himself suddenly whirled around and let out a yell. As Matt watched, Drang swooped forward and put both hard hands around the shoulders of a uniformed man who had been moving in the other direction.

His uniform was that of a North Vietnamese Army regular.

Matt hurried toward the lieutenant and his prey, worried by this first sign of North Viet interference and anxious to ask questions. He was framing the first one when he saw Drang's hands rise to the man's neck.

Matt called out, "No!"

It was too late. The North Vietnamese soldier fell to his knees. Dark as it was, Matt could see the man's face become white and then dark. He buckled, then lost his balance. Moans and gasps surged out from between his lips, and spittle stained his uniform. The spittle stopped, then, and there were no further moans. The soldier was dead by the time Drang let him go.

There was the innocent expectation of praise in Drang's attitude when he turned to Matt. "See?" he asked. "I killed him."

And at that moment a shell exploded less than twenty feet away. Matt, diving for cover, realized that he himself had probably given away the position this time by shouting.

Dave Lawlor had been running, the moon as his guide. He decided to take a shortcut toward the noise of firing, but the ground was more treacherous than it looked. He lost his balance and fell, rolling, to a point near what he realized had to be the mouth of a tunnel.

It offered a good chance to find out what Charlie's supplies were and a better chance to blow the place up

62

afterward. Besides, there might be some military information he could latch on to.

No sounds came from inside. Lawlor moved carefully, but couldn't help feeling like a sheep who knows it's being led to the butcher's meat grinder.

His left foot brushed past an obstacle, and he realized that he was in total darkness. With his eyes no good to him for a while, at least, his hearing became stronger than ever. He could make out a deep breath and a whispered curse. A footstep slithered along, not far from him.

Lawlor realized that he might be dealing with a scared South Vietnamese. Clearly and carefully he said, "I'm an American."

No response, except for the sound of a footstep. The darkness was inky black, and Lawlor knew he'd lose everything if he let himself become jittery. He had taken too much time coming in here. He ought to have blown the tunnel to pieces first and asked any questions whenever he could get around to it.

He flicked his knife open and held its back to his navel. In that position he'd be able to sink it into the gut of anybody who got close to him.

Think now, Lawlor told himself firmly, *whatever else you might want to do instead.* Those steps had come from about ten or twenty feet away, which meant that whoever was in here with him could be found at the far end of the tunnel sector. It was a good guess that whoever it was had been covering the door. Lawlor's own sense of direction was so shaky right now that he couldn't trust it and wasn't going to move. He wished he was up against a wall, but he'd have to do the best he could with whatever he was able to use in helping himself.

He was almost grateful that he could hear sounds of tight breaths drawn by whoever it was.

Lawlor decided to walk ahead, testing every step before putting his weight down on it. He took a couple of steps, then crashed into something hard and heavy and wooden. He pulled back abruptly, cursing under his breath. He supposed it was a table he had thunked against, and the damn thing had flopped over on a side into the dirt, taking any number of papers with it.

He could hear the sounds of gunfire outside now, but they were muffled. It was as if the whole fight were taking place inside a bottle.

Lawlor paused, crouching till he realized that the other guy wasn't likely to raise hell for a while. But he did hear the other guy take a deep, excited breath.

Lawlor decided on getting some advance warning in case the other guy tried coming closer. He managed to find the place where the table had fallen, then scattered most of the papers as far along the earth as he could manage without leaving the spot where he stood. If the other guy moved toward him now, Lawlor would hear the sheets rustle.

The other guy made his move before Lawlor could finish the job. He started forward, running this time. One of the sheets of paper crunched under a foot, but it wasn't Dave Lawlor's foot. The stirring air seemed to reach the hairs at the back of the sergeant's thick neck. At least he and the other guy weren't going to be playing cat-and-mouse inside a pitch-black tunnel.

The other guy called out suddenly, more of a gasp than a call, and surged forward. Lawlor used the knife. He heard a deeper gasp, and then the other guy fell.

Lawlor stabbed twice, the second time to the heart.

The guy was dead. No question about it.

Not until then was he able to use his flashlight and feel that he was safe. He pulled it out and lighted it. The beam fell across black pajamas and rose till he could see high breasts. For one of the few times in his life, Lawlor felt queasy.

He bent over. The girl was dead, for sure. Maybe she had been scared of him and had tried to get close to him toward the end, hoping that he would sense that she was a girl and think her harmless. Maybe she had become scared of a garter snake or some such and run toward him for help. Maybe she couldn't talk, or she'd have told him who she was and what she was.

Oh, he was brave all right. The hell he was.

Lawlor found the tunnel entrance and staggered toward it. He felt he couldn't do anything now. He, the natural-born fighter, was finished. He'd done his last killing. Let the SF hire him for pushing papers around a desk in the Pentagon if they still wanted him.

But the fresh air and the renewed sound of gunfire acted on him like a nerve tonic. He wondered if he had been dreaming things, back there. The VC women could be twice as dangerous as their men. That girl could have been leader of a cell, a dedicated girl who wanted to play cat-and-mouse with an American who'd accidentally found her hiding-place, and she had lost out.

By the time he was ten feet from the tunnel Lawlor realized that he never would know the answer and he'd be smart to spend no time worrying about it, but thinking only about the next Charlie. The way the action looked to him, there would be plenty of Charlies to keep him busy.

At least he damn well hoped so.

Jerry Garfine was in touch with the B team and asking for air strikes in the night sky and over areas he named. When the field telephone area came under VC attack, Garfine calmly moved away and took the unit with him. Just as he was fixing up to do some more sending, a pair of North Vietnamese soldiers appeared at the right of his field of vision. Garfine got the impression that he could keep quiet and get himself killed or send the message and get himself killed.

He began, "North Viets in town. Very close by."

As he talked he was fumbling with his shirt, and he suddenly wheeled around and threw a grenade. One of the North Viet soldiers caught it squarely in the gut. The other one ducked and fired.

The bullet grazed Jerry Garfine's arm. He let loose a grenade with his good hand. The number-two North Viet was gone, too, either dead or vanished.

Garfine pulled out a handkerchief and held it against his left arm, but while he was taking care of the injury he kept talking into the field telephone.

"Looks like a nice party shaping up," he said calmly. "Try and send some guys over for the fun, if they've got any free time. And by the way, they'll have to bring their own cocktails. The best brand of cocktail out here is that good Russian stuff called Molotov."

Seven

VICTOR FRASER sat patiently behind the wheel of his two-tone Jaguar on Kan Roh Street in nighttime Saigon. He was an ugly man with big ears, a squashed nose, hard eyes, and thick lips. His hair had become iron-gray during twelve years in this city, but not an attractive shade of gray. Glasses perched on his nose like twin cannon at the sides of a hill. His suit, shirt, tie, and shoes were British, and he tried to wear the outfit as if he had grown into it.

He heard the arrogant cr-rackle of high-heeled footsteps and looked out through the car's spotless windshield. His heart gave a lurch so sudden that he felt dizzy. She was turning in to this street and flashing sex at every man who saw her, a small but high-breasted blond in her mid-twenties and at the peak of her physical attractiveness.

She stepped into the Pinot Hotel, and Fraser got out of the car, locked it, and followed. He found her in the bar, sitting on a stool and talking to the bartender. Fraser never knew how he managed to introduce himself to women, being so conscious of his ugliness, but he did it somehow. This woman gave her name as Evelyn Colbert. She wore a wedding ring. Fraser felt a sudden stabbing pain at the point where the bridge of his nose disappeared into his forehead.

"I don't suppose," he floundered.

"You can buy me a drink, but that's all." Evelyn Colbert smiled, briefly crinkling the perfect white skin around her eyes.

"Of course," Fraser said. "I assume your husband is in the service."

"He is, yes."

Fraser tapped a breast pocket and gave a relieved half smile. "Well, let's get a table, shall we? My first name is Victor, by the way."

Fraser thought that every man in the place turned around to follow Evelyn Colbert's progress as she marched to one of the tables. And he thought that those same men looked at him with a mocking envy that he had seen a few times before when he was out with a pretty young woman.

The table talk was light and easygoing.

"I suppose you're a wheeler-dealer by trade," Evelyn Colbert said, smiling over her White Russian.

"Who isn't?"

He had touched his jacket pocket again, and she said, "I notice you doing that all the time."

"I keep my passport there," he lied.

"Well, you shouldn't practically point to it the way you're doing," Evelyn Colbert said. "Oh!"

Fraser had managed to tilt her drink very slightly so that several drops spilled out on her dress. Evelyn Colbert stood up and hurried out to the ladies' room.

Fraser didn't waste time when she was gone. He pulled Evelyn's drink over to him and made a pyramid with one hand, covering what he did with the other. He used that one to inch out the envelope, open it, spill some powder into the dark drink, and then swizzle the result. In his hurry he came close to spilling part of it again. He was smiling slightly when he put the drink back in front of Evelyn Colbert's place.

She came back and finished the drink and sat and talked to him. He didn't tell much about himself, and she said very little, maybe because she was used to thinking that it wasn't good to talk about Matt's movements when he was in a war situation.

She started to wipe her brow with a perfumed handkerchief and her face was becoming red. "I'll go for a walk," she said suddenly. "I'm not feeling too well."

"Let me go with you," Fraser said smoothly. "Or better yet, let's take a ride in my car."

"Will it be safe?"

"Of course. I wouldn't suggest it otherwise."

"Whatever we do, I can't stand it inside here for another minute. That drink really knocked me out."

She breathed heavily when she got into the car, then let down the window on her side and gulped warm air. Her mouth was wide-open as Fraser drove, and she couldn't seem to stop wiping her face. The warm air annoyed Fraser, but his opinion hadn't been asked.

"Are you all right now?"

"No, I'm not."

"I'll drive around till you feel better."

"Take me to a doctor instead. I really don't feel well at all, and I want to—"

She started to nod determinedly, but didn't finish. Her eyes suddenly opened very wide. Her entire body shook in a spasm, and then she fell sideways against him. She looked unconscious.

Fraser swore. Once in his life he had tried to get a pretty woman for himself, using some of the stuff that a druggist had sold him as a sure way to get a woman excited; and instead he had given her too much of the stuff and she was dead to the world.

Dead? She couldn't be!

Fraser rested her against the shoulder of the seat she had taken. She looked so quiet that he couldn't make out the sight of her stomach drawing in and popping out again. He put a palm less than a quarter of an inch from her stomach, and realized that her stomach hadn't touched it. Not till he checked for her pulse did he finally tell himself he couldn't feel any.

She was dead.

Now that his problem didn't involve the reactions of a woman, Fraser felt that he was in better control than before. He was irritable when the body swayed against him in the night traffic and he had to wait for the next signal before moving it from direct contact with him. When he saw a policeman directing traffic later on he felt annoyed with the man for being there. It didn't occur to Fraser that he himself had done anything wrong.

He'd have to work out an effective lie or some way of hiding the real cause of death. There wouldn't be much investigation if he worked it right. Not in a war-torn town like this one. Fraser's smile didn't leave his face any less ugly than usual.

He suddenly nodded, having been struck by what seemed like a fine notion. He'd have liked to take a sheet of paper and draw a line down the middle, then mark faults on one side and advantages on the other, numbering every point that might occur to him on either side and studying the results.

He drove past Tu Do Street, with its exclusive Caravelle Hotel, and circled the American Embassy, which looked to him like a fort under siege. He passed the place farther on in which war profiteers had used to be publicly shot by the Diem government, and the black-market area where people dealt mostly in supplies stolen from U.S. installations. He was headed for a fairly deserted section of town, deserted except for occasional roving bands of troublemakers.

Fraser stopped near a rise and went to work on the plan he had hit on while he was coming out here.

His first move was to search Evelyn Colbert's pocketbook by the dashboard light and take everything out of it that night be valuable. A cigarette case, a wallet, and a change purse were the items he took and dropped into a pocket handkerchief. Searching his own pockets for valuables, he added his wallet and some change, a gold fountain pen, and his own cigarette case to the pile. He tied the oversized handkerchief at its ends, then got out of the car and walked a short distance. Then he leaned over and buried the stuff in a patch of soft earth.

70

The first part of his plan was finished. The easiest part.

Back in the car he tore Evelyn Colbert's dress from the top at one point and from the bottom at another. He crinkled her underclothes, and almost shredded the half slip. Then he mussed her fine-spun hair. With a paper tissue he later threw out as far as it'd go, he smeared her lipstick to the sides of her well-formed lips and a bit under them. With a fist he hit the dead woman below the eyes. Twice he did it.

The next part was going to be rougher on him, because he had to make himself look like a victim too. First he rumpled his hair, then creased part of a shirt cuff with his hand. Laying himself down on the floor he rolled from left to right as far as he could and then back again. He had to keep his knees up because the car wasn't big enough, and he had to push the dead woman's legs out toward the lower panel, but he got it done. Dirt was as good as printed on him now.

Next he took off his glasses and coldly crushed one lens underfoot. With a grunt that didn't hide distaste for what he was doing, Fraser hit his head against the floor. Again he lifted his body, took a deep breath, and slammed it down hard. He used all the force in him. Three more times he did it before he was satisfied. Either that, or too groggy to think any longer.

But he opened the nearest door, groggy or not, then opened the other one. While he was at it, Evelyn Colbert's body slipped and moved toward the right, touching the horn. Fraser pulled it away quickly. It was his plan to walk out, get help, and then let the whole business be settled by the police. Settled, of course, the way he wanted it done.

No, there wasn't a single hole in his plan. The evidence was on his side every bit of the way. Any damn fool of a policeman would take it for granted what had happened. Evelyn Colbert's death would be figured as the result of a mugging. Not the first one in this section, heaven knew, and not likely to be the last.

71

He was getting out of the car the best way he could manage when he heard a murmur close by. Two people were talking. The hushed voices carried this far only on account of the quiet around them.

Fraser didn't understand Vietnamese except for a few words, but it struck him that the tone these men took was very quiet and taut. It was as if each man was holding himself under great control.

They came into sight at last, two thin, hard-eyed men. They carried clubs with the point of a nail through the far end of each one. Fraser had only a moment to realize that Evelyn Colbert's head falling across the car horn had signaled these men that some possible victims were in the neighborhood again, and then the two men fell upon him.

The fight was short. For Fraser it was fatal.

She was cold and sick and miserable. Those were her first feelings when she realized that she felt anything at all.

Worst of all, it seemed to her, she was lying down in dirt.

Evelyn Colbert stirred. She was numb from the legs down, or at least that was how it seemed. She actually felt for her pulse and wasn't surprised that it was faint. For the first few seconds or so, she'd have sworn that there wasn't any pulse at all.

She could hear a car being driven away and didn't know or care that she had been thrown out of it only a little while before.

As she stood up, she tried to remember what had happened. There had been an ugly fellow who had bought her a drink, and some of the drink had tasted funny, and after that she'd started to feel a little queasy and he had suggested taking a ride with him.

And then she supposed he had made a pass and she had said no and he'd knocked her out and left her in the dirt and driven away.

She knew now that never again was she going to get

mixed up with any man except her husband. Not even in a casual way at a bar. Not even to talk to. She was thankful that since her marriage she had never gone to bed with any man but the one she'd married.

Luckily she didn't see the dead body on the earth. It would have broken her down completely. She was able to make out a string of lights over the rise of the hill and a few hundred yards past it. Evelyn Colbert gathered as much of the dress together as she could and started for those lights.

Dek Ho Quan had paid for the cigarettes with a battered piaster note. The cashier looked down at it, then folded it lengthwise with a creaking thumbnail and muttered that a boy of his age shouldn't be smoking.

"Thank you," Dek Ho said in English.

It was one of the many English phrases he knew. At fourteen he was able to earn a living selling stolen monkeys to soldiers in front of billets. It was a fair living, but his father made more money working at the Cho Lon docks.

Dek Ho glanced back of the cashier at the mirror and saw himself, big for fourteen as he was already five feet tall, and careful to dress neatly. He brushed a speck from the top of a shoulder and held out both hands as if he wanted to show the mirror how clean they were. He looked clean too, and for a boy who lived in Saigon these days that was pretty unusual.

He could never sell monkeys at night, so he'd generally go home and wash himself. He didn't usually know where the elder Quan might be, and he hardly ever cared. He always knew where to find the elder Quan when he had to. As soon as he felt clean once more he would go to a small pad and pencil he kept near his bed and write down the day and date on it and next to that the number of piasters he had earned.

He was going to become a doctor someday. He'd get enough money to go to a school, and when he was finished with that he would help his people in Saigon and in the provinces. He would become a very rich man. In the meantime he smoked and tried to figure out new ways of making money.

He was wearing his only suit when he walked toward the park late that night. Nobody ever knew who might be in the neighborhood and might want or need help and be willing to pay for it. Dek Ho Quan was seldom bothered by hoodlums in the park. He was known, and he hardly ever carried more than half a dozen p-notes in his pockets at one time.

And one never knew what a doctor-to-be might learn about grownups. The world was a mystery, and some clues might be found in a quiet place where you could sit and think, for a while at least.

Dek Ho was sitting on a rock when he saw the woman. She was white and she was running. Her dress was torn and he told himself that it was impossible to see her without feeling pity.

"Are you well?" He spoke in English.

"I—" The woman looked at him. She drew a deep breath and her lips stretched into a smile. "I've had some trouble."

"Your dress is torn," he said. "There are bad people in the park. No woman should go here when is—uh . . ."

"Alone," Evelyn Colbert said automatically. "By herself."

"Yes, alone." Dek Ho smiled. "English is a difficult language."

"Did you learn it at school?"

Dek Ho had never been in a school, but he nodded gravely and said, "A little."

Evelyn Colbert hesitated. She needed a few minutes to clear her senses, and this boy represented human society.

He said, "Let us walk together outside and to the city. You will feel much better, I think."

"Yes," she said gratefully, and began to walk. Dek Ho felt her soft breath touch the back of his neck.

74

Partly to make conversation, she asked him, "What do you study in school?"

"I study to be a doctor when I am big. I will help people."

She said gently, "You should start by helping yourself. Smoking is not the way to do that. Don't your parents tell you to stop smoking?"

"Yes." Dek Ho had never seen his mother and would almost have bet his medical-school money that she had never gone through a wedding ceremony with his father. the elder Quan was too fond of many, many women to let himself be roped to one. Hardly a night went by that the elder Quan wasn't bringing home a woman.

This child was funny, Evelyn Colbert thought. He dressed like the little bridegroom on a wedding cake, but he had big, bulging eyes and fingers that moved like snakes growing out of his hands. He didn't look like anybody she had ever seen or known.

When they got to the end of the park area, the night's automatic firing had started, and Evelyn held her hands to her ears. The boy grinned in a superior way.

He said to her, "Your dress is bad. You may have trouble if you're seen in this way."

"Yes. Yes, that's true."

"My house is a short way from here," he said. "Come with me."

She blinked. "What do you mean?"

"I can get dress for you from woman who lives in house near ours."

"Yes, I suppose your mother could do that. But why should she do it for a stranger?"

Dek Ho didn't look at her but said, "I will see to everything."

He smiled. His intention was kind, and he wanted only to be of some help. Evelyn had never seen a nicer boy, certainly not at a time when she was in distress.

The walk was a short one, only two blocks. Dek Ho lived in a one-story house that looked to Evelyn as if it

75

had been made of paper. Windows were dirty, and she wondered what sort of housekeeper the mother could be.

He opened the door for her, then stood to one side and let her walk in.

She did, trying hard to show that fish smells in this house didn't bother her at all. Something else soon took her mind from the smell.

"There's no woman here," she said. "There couldn't be. The woman isn't born who'd let her house be so disorderly. You've lied to me!"

The noise must have attracted the elder Quan, because the door opened on a graying man who scratched his day-old beard. He looked at Evelyn and grinned, giving the look that Dek Ho realized was lustful. Then he turned to the boy.

"You've brought something good," he said in Vietnamese, and lunged toward Evelyn. He reached her and put both arms around her, then covered her mouth with one of his hands. Evelyn's voice was muffled and her heels beat a tattoo on the floor till Dek Ho's father suddenly bent over and picked her up over a shoulder and took her into his room.

Dek Ho knew better than to interfere with his father. He had tried it before and been badly beaten every time. He stood in the darkness, fists clenced and cursing softly, then a little more loudly to help cover the sounds coming from the bedroom. He could hear the sounds over cannon fire as clothes were being mauled and muffled words spoken, the woman pleading and then crying.

Dek Ho had decided that he'd wait and try to convince the woman that he wasn't to blame and then take her back to her home or lodging. He hadn't known what was going to happen, and he wanted her to believe it.

The bedroom door opened heavily. His father, shirt off and pants zipped open, lumbered out. He was smiling widely, showing the gaps in his teeth. A soft murmur from the bedroom faded slightly on account of the woman's hoarseness.

"You have done me a service, and you deserve some-

76

thing for it," the elder Quan said, reaching into his pants pockets and coming out with twenty piaster notes.

"The night has only begun," the elder Quan said as he turned around and walked back into the bedroom again, closing the door behind him.

With all the woman's crying, Dek Ho doubted whether he'd be able to sleep in the house for this night. Usually it was laughter or shouts that he heard from his father's bedroom at night, and those sounds he could live with; but not this.

Dek Ho put away the twenty p's in his hiding-place and went outside. At first he walked slowly, but what with the high excitement of gunfire and the knowledge that he'd picked up twenty piasters he hadn't expected, his mood changed. Those twenty p's would help see him through the school of medicine, Dek Ho decided, mentally earmarking them for the purpose. Those twenty piasters were going to let him help the people of Vietnam. Indeed, when he became a doctor he would be of service to all mankind.

Dek Ho whistled under his breath as he walked.

Eight

It was slightly past dawn in the Tam Hung area, and the men who survived carried with them what was left of their C-ration packs and canteens along with rifles, grenades, and entrenching tools. Not many of them had slept.

Ken Hubbard woke up in a ridge where he could see dried shredded Marine flak jackets and fatigues from a recent battle in this same area. Down the side of the road was a skull on a stake. At the bottom of the stake a note written with blood on cardboard said, WE BE BACK.

A soldier stumbled past, a wounded man on his shoulders. Ken could hear an occasional round of sniper fire but not much else. He knew he stank; so did the clothes on his back. He wished he knew exactly where in hell he was.

Matt Colbert had slept in a sitting position under a banyan at the side of a rutted road. He got up quickly when a Viet soldier nudged him. Before he had blinked his eyes twice, he remembered everything and wished he had left more of the men back at base. He had wanted to feel sure there would be enough men back there to guide any replacements in taking over, but nothing could be done about it now. He was reaching for field glasses as he stood up and peered out to where the enemy must be waiting to strike again or maybe getting set to take more casualties in another SF attack.

Jerry Garfine had been on patrol for half the night and had run into nothing but false alarms. The left arm, where he'd been nicked yesterday, itched a little but didn't keep him from working. He'd practically forgotten about it already.

Corporal Overby was on his way back to the lines, having led half a dozen Viet soldiers on a scouting patrol. They had scored an ambush, killing ten North Viet regulars and netting three AKV-47 Chicom rifles.

When he took the leadership of a patrol like this one, Overby would put on his Sedang bead necklace and his Jeh brass bracelets, because it made the men feel better to know that they'd be in the hands of somebody who had been accepted as a brother by the Jeh tribesmen. In a little while he would be joining the men as they sat around and chewed sugar cane and drank some of that rice wine that they flipped over. To Overby the stuff tasted like liquid cement, the sugar cane was too sweet to his palate, and the jewelry was a Goddamn pain in the butt.

The perils of pacification, he thought to himself. The Americans with whom he worked would have been surprised to know that the only corporal on their A team had a streak of humor in his nature.

Soldier talk among the men under fire was a luxury in which most of them couldn't take part for longer than a couple of minutes at a time.

"This Goddamn action will keep going till I retire," one man complained.

"Me, too. Can you imagine the next fifteen years cooped up in Tam Hung?"

"You know what's wrong with you, pal? You just don't like Charlie, that's what wrong with you."

"You're kidding!"

"Hell, no. You're too Goddamn hostile and aggressive. That's why you carry a Goddamn gun around with you.

You got to realize Charlie had a poor bringing up and his mother didn't understand him."

"All I want to is get out of here, that's all."

"You? Hell, you're a Green Beret, man, the elite action force. You love danger. You chew broken bottles for breakfast—or don't you ever read that stuff in the papers about how brave you are? There's even a song about you."

"Stop the crap, will you? Listen, when I get out of the army, I'm going to buy a farm and live on the money I get paid not to grow crops. You can't beat that for an angle. I won't never travel again, except to the bedroom or the bathroom."

"Not even Hong Kong?"

"When I get out of the army, I won't even piss on Hong Kong if it gets on fire."

"You know what I figure I'll do afterwards? I'll sink some money into the stock market and see what happens."

"You'll lose your ass, that's what'll happen. Some broker will cut off your nuts so you can invest 'em and get four, only you'll never even have the two you were born with."

"Is that right? Well, you guys will be standing out on street corners selling shoelaces and I'll be driving to my broker's office in a fur-covered Cadillac. Just you guys wait and you'll see who turns into a millionai——"

"Hey! Charlie's shooting like he means business, and I think he's coming around through them bushes."

"Okay, you can make your million some other time. Better shoot the ass off Charlie now."

The sniper fire would start and stop and then start again. Machine-gun fire would answer it in stutters of sound, and then the sniper attack would pick up from another point.

Ken Hubbard had blasted a clearing back of a stand of bushes and then dug a hole five feet deep and seven feet wide. The job took him an hour and a half, and he got some help from his Viet counterpart, Han Ho

Diam. When the job was finished, Han Ho joined him. He was about two finger-joints taller than Ken but not nearly as thin, and his hands were powerful. With a little more patience, he might have been a first-class soldier. Ken had always been told that Asians were the patient ones while Yanks insisted that everything get done yesterday, but Han Ho Diam didn't seem to know any of the rules.

Tension was riding Hubbard and his throat was tight, but he said quietly, "Any sniper who misses this spot in front of us is a fool. When he comes, there'll be a surprise waiting for him."

"Good. I stay and kill."

With Han Ho's help, Ken covered most of the hole with log roofing and troweled mud on top of it with his entrenching tool. When he was ready he used TNT to blast away a line of bushes back of them, giving the snipers a better view of the clearing.

A mortar attack had started up from Charlie's territory, and Ken could hear familiar voices calling for medic help. It was too dangerous for him to leave, so he crawled into the hole with Han Ho.

It took very little time before Charlie decided to use the clearing section, but not for the purpose that Ken and Han Ho had hoped. They started putting their dead down in it and near the hole. The smell of decomposing flesh and garbage was enough to make Ken nauseous, but he kept looking out.

"We'll take watch-and-watch," Ken decided. "Fifteen minutes for you and the same for me. All right?"

"Very good."

But the smell of death was nearly as persistent to Ken during the time he leaned back and shut his eyes and tried to think about other things. There didn't seem to be any other things, though. Not now.

He felt Han Ho's body become stiff with anger before the Vietnamese counterpart said a word.

Ken peered out. A man in a North Viet uniform caked

81

with mud was approaching the clearing's end and crouching as he looked through it at the Special Forces side. The enemy sniper suddenly turned and made a gesture in the direction of his fellow soldiers. It was the universal come-here sweep with one outstretched arm bending at the elbow.

Han Ho raised his rifle.

Ken put a hand on him. "Wait."

"He is here," Han Ho said, annoyance deepening his tones. "Now I kill him."

"He signaled for other men to join him," Ken whispered urgently. "If we hold off, we'll land others, too."

The enemy soldier sighted and then fired a couple of times. He glanced around once, probably wondering why the other men hadn't joined him by this time.

Han Ho said quickly, "He fires on our men, mine and yours. There are twenty of mine to every one of yours. I can't let my men be killed."

Ken pointed out, "He can't be killing or wounding with every shot."

"How do you know?"

Ken put a finger to his lips, hoping that Han Ho would at least be quieter. Han Ho obliged but sighted through his GI rifle. There would be no way of stopping the crazy fool.

Han Ho fired. The sniper wheeled around, surprise etched on his face, then fell dead.

A number of bullets sprayed the hole in which the two men were crouched. Han Ho Diam gasped and was dead before Ken could do anything more than move to lay himself out flat. He covered his body with Han Ho's. Bullets sang over him.

In a few minutes the log covering had been torn away. Ken sensed the daylight as Viet soldiers looked down and saw, he hoped, one body. They argued for a little while, and then Ken felt pressure as part of the dead body seemed to become heavier against him. It drew away, and then another part of the dead body felt as if it was being squeezed against his back. It happened twice more before Ken realized that the dead South Vietnamese was being mercilessly bayoneted. If the bayonet wounds went much deeper, he knew that he himself would be gutted like a fish.

There was a sudden machine-gun barrage overhead, and the pressures against Ken suddenly stopped. He supposed that the North Vietnamese firing at the hole had pinpointed their location and were now under attack from the Special Forces men.

He never knew how much time passed as he lay under a dead man and smelled decomposing bodies and knew he had better not move. Ken Hubbard had always considered himself a patient man, but he wanted to scream and scream. He didn't know if anybody was near the body above him, so he didn't do a thing.

It took twenty minutes to shift himself slightly without being detected. The dead man was closer to him than before if his sense of smell was a good guide; and he could see the back of one of Han Ho's hands. As sunlight shifted Ken knew the day was wearing on. When he could hardly make out the hand any more, he knew that night had fallen. He didn't suppose he'd ever be more safe.

Cautiously, he moved. He managed to ease the body over on one side and was able to look at what seemed a moonless sky. He raised himself slightly, but the pain took him by surprise and he cursed. Twigs crackled on the ground as a soldier rushed over to the hole. Ken couldn't get to the M-16 on time.

A voice said in English, "Thought that was you, Sergeant."

"Overby!" Ken nearly shouted with relief. "Have we got this ground now?"

"We've had it since the morning."

"God! And I've been lying under a dead man while I could've got up and danced not had any trouble."

"Charlie fires at us sometimes, you know, Sergeant,"

Overby said with what Ken assumed was his usual stolidity. "We'd better get your friend out of there just in case we need a hole for ourselves."

"He's been through it," Ken said gruffly, looking down at Han Ho. "Let him rest."

But when he heard blast number one of a new mortar attack, Ken practically threw himself back into the hole. Overby landed on top of him, hitting Ken in the back. Mortar shells thundered and rumbled around the hole, adding the smell of burnt powder to that of decomposing flesh. Ken wasn't able to move or breathe without having a hard time over it.

The attack lasted for six or seven minutes, by his guess. When Overby got up gingerly, Ken joined him. The body of Han Ho Diam, which had been in the hole with them, flopped out to nearly the length of the hole. Ken saw then that the dead man's head had been cut off at the neck by shrapnel. He shuddered at the narrow escape, never having expected he'd be grateful to share a hole with a dead man.

"Poor bastard," he muttered. "Charlie has sure got it in for him."

"The choppers will get here soon," the first soldier said.

"It don't matter," the second soldier said with difficulty. "I've had it. I crapped out."

"Ah, hell, you've got yourself a million-dollar cut, that's all. Lay back and relax. You don't know what trouble is."

"I've had it, I tell you. I know."

"Well, I thought I'd had it too, once, but you never really know. Back home one time, I was sure I'd be going to jail, but I went into the Special Forces instead and I haven't got a record. You think you've got trouble. If I tell you what happened to me that time with one broad, you'll know what trouble really is."

"Leave me alone, will you? I know you're trying to

84

help me feel a little better, but nobody can do a thing."

"Listen, will you? It's pretty funny in a way, I guess. I remember how I felt on top of the world one afternoon when I got out of the offices of the First Mutual Savings and Loan Association back in—Jesus, that was close! Charlie's hitting real good today."

"You're damn right."

"Anyway I went out of the office with twenty thousand bucks in my jacket pocket, and there was a blond waiting for me when I was two blocks away. I can remember it like it happened last night. Crystal, her name was. High heels, big boobies, the works. She was smiling, but in a nervous way.

"I said to her, 'Did you get it?'

"She pointed down to the small pocketbook she was lugging around with her. 'I did it for you,' she said, 'because I couldn't stand to lose you. I took twenty thous—— I don't want to say it or even think about it any more.'

"Well, I told her all over again that the certain race I knew about had been fixed and not one bookie in town had got the straight story. The plan was to bet the money in different places and make a killing. I wanted her to bet it, and she finally said she would. After all she was prettier than me, and the biggies might not get so bugged about certain bets if a pretty girl made the bets."

"I don't want to hear this. I'll never hear anything ag——"

"You're just shook up, that's all. So Crystal said, 'I wish I could hold back on anything you want,' and did the betting. We went home and had us a great night, me and her."

"I'll never get laid again."

"Shut up and listen, will you? The race was going to be run next day, a Saturday, and I caught it on the TV. Crystal was sitting next to me, sexy as anything, but it didn't make no difference. I wasn't in the mood. Not then.

85

"My horse was called Sunburst, and on the last turn he was nose-to-nose with another nag. It was a photo finish, which I knew was what had been planned. In a few minutes the announcer says that the winning horse is called King's Ransom. You get that? The other horse had won.

"Later on I found out that the horse had suddenly put too much stress on one leg and pitched forward, so the win was an accident. But that wouldn't cut any ice with the Savings and Loan people I worked for. I ran out of the house without a word to Crystal and started trying to raise money to put back. I only had to borrow twenty thousand dollars, because Crystal, I figured, could take care of herself. I knew it'd take me years to pay back at the six-for-five rate, but I couldn't help it.

"So the next day I go to work—Monday, this was, now, of course—and fix up the account sheets. My boss, Mr. Shevlin, saw me working like forked lightning, and he smiled.

"'There seems to be a trend toward ambition today,' the creep said. 'It makes me want to examine the books right now.'

"I figured he could go spit up a rope for all I cared. When I left I saw Crystal on the top step of the vault and heard her talking to me when I was on the—"

"It won't be long," the second soldier gasped out. "I'm dying, I tell you!"

"When I was on the way upstairs," the first soldier continued more loudly, "what she said got me all shook up. You'll hear. She said, 'Don't worry about anything. I didn't let the worst happen. I put back the money you had taken along with my own. I couldn't bring myself to make those bets. I knew you might get mad, but I couldn't do it.'

"'Goddammit,' I said. 'Thanks to you, my accounts are twenty thousand *over*, and Shevlin is sure to—'"

The second soldier said with a little more liveliness, "Don't shit a crap artist, man. I know that's a lot of

86

malarkey, and it never could happen that way. You're making it up and—"

"Harry! Harry, for Chrissake, what's wrong? Don't look like that, Harry! All right, all right, I made it up. I figured for sure you'd get a charge out of it. Harry, for Chrissake I admit the whole thing. I'm a liar, see? I admit I'm a liar, Harry! I admit it. You hear?"

The soldier called Harry was never going to hear anything again, and the first soldier finally realized it. But he had to be given a shot to make him quiet down, and he was sent back to base in one of the first returning choppers.

The battle had been going on for thirty-one hours. Special Forces had lost sixty-eight men and won a hundred yards of territory. Enemy losses amounted to well over two hundred killed and wounded. To Special Forces, the engagement would be known as a victory. To the relatives of sixty-eight men it would always be a defeat.

The first chopper hovered in the air while a basket was lowered to take the first of the wounded. A burst of ground fire drove the pilot away for a time. A grenade had taken care of the source of gunfire by the time that pilot came back again, but this time he radioed that the air was too thin for him to hover, and he vanished from sight. On his third try, one man was hoisted up successfully.

Chris Ablett, first lieutenant on the A team, who had been cross-trained as a medic, turned away sourly when the helicopter rose with its human cargo.

"I'd be surprised if he's alive for another half hour," he said darkly.

Two more choppers appeared, to haul out wounded men. Ablett's face was drawn as he supervised the work. Matt Colbert, seeing his second-in-command, instinctively kept from looking into hard gray eyes that had seen far too much in the last few hours.

Matt said instantly, "We've done as much damage as Okinawa could expect, Matt, and we'll be clearing out soon."

"It won't be too soon," Chris Ablett remarked.

Ken Hubbard and Overby had been put to work carving a landing zone out of jungle area. They used twenty-pound charges of TNT. After digging for a few minutes, one of them would step back and yell to everybody in earshot, "Hit the dirt!"

Men scrambled for cover before the explosion. Hubbard and Overby would nearly always be covered with dust and tree bark when the explosion was done, but while Hubbard sneezed and wiped the gook off him the corporal would simply get back to work.

The two of them had been at it so hard that neither man noticed how much darker it was becoming. Ken Hubbard finally realized that he couldn't see the watch on his left wrist and said to Overby, "There's too much Goddamn crap in the air."

Overby squinted up at the sky. Ken's eyes turned to follow, but he stopped himself when he made out Matt Colbert coming toward them. The captain's jaw was set, and his lips looked like thin slashes on a wooden surface.

"When do you expect you'll be finished?"

"An hour, Captain. Tops."

"Do you want help to get the job done faster?"

"No, sir. It won't do any good." Ken asked quietly, "Is Charlie still raising hell?"

"Charlie we can handle. The weather we can't."

For the first time Ken looked up and saw the swollen black-edged clouds over his head.

"Rain, sir?"

"What the hell do *you* think?" Matt growled. "If we get caught here in the rain we'll drown. Every last damn one of us."

Ken Hubbard didn't excuse himself to the captain but wheeled around abruptly and went back to work.

Matt looked away. Choppers were coming over pretty

fast now, dumping ammunition and water and taking out casualties. Bodies of men killed in action were being loaded on board some of the choppers. A fierce down-draft blew off one of the ponchos. Matt took time to put it back in place and kept from looking at what was left of one man.

Nine

NINA FIELD hadn't told anybody, with one exception, about the harm she'd had to do to another human being by destroying his face. She'd had to talk about it to that strange-looking fellow at the American Embassy, but nobody else was going to know.

She was dressing for dinner with two friends who worked for AID and had a small home in Northeast Saigon. She had promised herself this night out, and her dark attractiveness had never shown to better effect.

When she left the hospital for the evening she didn't plan to make any stopovers, but halfway to her destination she suddenly told the driver to stop while she went into a food store. She bought some fruits and vegetables and had them put into little bags and then asked the storekeeper to drop them into a huge bag half as big as she was. The driver carried all of it out to the cab.

Nina said, "Take me to the poorest section of town."

The driver shrugged but did what she wanted. Nina took half a dozen of the small bags with her when she stepped out, telling the driver that she had written down his license number and if he tried to get away with the packages she would make sure he was arrested.

She was in a section where ragged huts had been built out of cardboard and tin. Children scampered around, but the older people looked tired and drawn. An old man was sitting cross-legged in the door of one hut. Nina pressed one of the packages on him, and the old man's face twisted. Salty tears seeped down from the corners of his big eyes. Then he sank his head into his hands and rocked back and forth. Not one word had been said between them, and Nina very much preferred it that way. What could she tell the man, after all? She was trying to help him and some other people who looked very bad, and that was all there was to it.

She gave another food package to a woman pacing back and forth in front of one of the huts, a wooden stump held in her mouth instead of a cigarette. Another package went to a middle-aged man who sat on a rickety chair, nails digging into his arms. The man wouldn't take her gift in hand, so Nina left it at his side. He drew his nails down toward a spot just over his elbows as she watched, then dug them in viciously.

Still another package was given to a girl with a runny nose, and her fifth package went to a tall, pimply boy. Then she went back to the cab for more packages.

A crowd had formed, and she found herself giving away some packages to people who looked as if they had been eating pretty well recently. She was glad when there were no more packages left and she gestured that her hands were empty. The crowd became sullen and then a little angry. Nina had the impression that her cab was going to be overturned by some of the people who hadn't been given any packages.

The driver, cursing everybody in his path, finally got the cab away and out of danger at last. He was probably cursing Nina as much as anybody on the street for all she knew, her understanding of Vietnamese being as slight as it was.

She mentioned her gift-giving experience to Fred and Janice Pierce when she reached the house where the two of them were staying. She added that, unpleasant as it had been, she felt she had made up a little for the harm she'd had to do on the day before.

"Giving away food packages on an impromptu basis in this town is a mistake," Fred remarked, laughing good-naturedly as he leaned across the kitchen table. He was a man with bushy hair and thick eyebrows, and he wore a light suit that looked as if it had been glued onto his ungainly body. "I can understand why you did it, Nina.

91

It's hard to be so close to human suffering without trying to help a little. But in this setup it's a mistake."

"Tell me why."

"If the world is against you, Nina, you become angry
and resentful at people who have got so much of the
world's goods that they can afford to throw it away."

Janice said, "Refugees are never grateful, dear." She
was in her late twenties, a mouse-blond who rarely went
in for backbiting. She worked well with her husband on
small local AID projects. "They can make things very
diffic——"

She cocked her head to one side when the doorbell
rang, then answered it. When she came back in a couple
of minutes she looked puzzled. "A local is out there," she
said. "He's so—so dirty that I asked him to wait outside.
He said that the woman who just came in here owes
him something."

Nina didn't show that she was surprised, but she did
look at Fred. He had been putting a napkin between his
shirt collar and neck, but now he bounced up from the
chair and ran over to the closed door past the living
room. Nina, puzzled, looked over at Janice.

"I couldn't get a straight story from him," Janice admitted. "Did you promise him some food and not give
it to him?"

"I didn't make any promises. I didn't talk to anybody,
Janice. I just gave out the packages."

They heard Fred slam the door severely, then test it
twice to make sure it was locked. He strode into the
washroom before rejoining his wife and Nina.

"I had to kick him out," he explained, coming back.
"He says you were supposed to give him some food,
Nina."

Nina controlled herself, but never knew how she managed it.

"I didn't promise anybody anything!"

"Probably not, but how that guy on foot was able to
follow a cab . . . Well, I guess it couldn't happen that

way any other place in the world except in Saigon traffic."

"Did you give him something to get rid of him?"

"If I did that, me and Janice would never have a quiet moment," Fred said grimly. "God knows I sympathize with every one of them, but I have a lot more sympathy for me and my wife. Refugees need help desperately and they know you know it, so they expect help as a matter of right and they become like employees with tenure, if you know what I mean."

A soft knocking was heard at the door. Fred's right hand was making a fist when he hurried to answer it. The door opened and was closed again quickly. Fred strode back into the kitchen, his brows drawn down.

"A woman this time," he said. "So help me God, Nina, you really got a couple of dolls on your track. I said no to her and used some profanity and sent her on her way."

Nina said, "I'm sorry I got you into this."

"Everybody makes mistakes out here and has got to learn," Janice said. "I remember once when I—"

The doorbell again. Fred took that short walk to the door again, shouted through it, and walked back.

"I promised I'd kill the next person who rings the bell or knocks," he growled. "That ought to finish it."

Janice nodded once, then suddenly stood and walked over to the nearest window. She raised the shade. Her breath started to come heavily. Nina, startled, joined her.

Men and women, tired, bedraggled, unhappy, were crossing the street or reaching the sidewalk and talking to others. Every eye strayed to the door, then the window. Seeing the two women, they approached, old men and women as well as younger people and children, hands up in pleading as words fell from their shaky lips.

Fred, standing just behind his wife and their friend, was white-faced. He looked away toward the kitchen table.

It was impossible to think or talk in the small, overheated kitchen. Nina could hear what must have been ragged desperate jokes and pained cries that carried through the closed window.

93

The street seemed black with people who probably took up every inch of space. Fred shook a fist at them, but nobody moved and nothing changed.

Brown-uniformed police appeared among the crowd, listening and using clubs when it seemed necessary. Slowly the crowd began to thin out. Nina, her face white and shaken, watched the nightmare that seemed to have come to life in front of her.

Several minutes went by before she felt calm enough to look back at her friends again. She would have given anything in the world not to feel as useless as she did right now, but there was no help for it in this house or the nearest hospital. Vietnam in the north and south was made up of people who felt as if they were caught on a treadmill, but she had never realized it as clearly as she did now.

"Well now," Janice said brightly, "what say we sit down and finish dinner, huh?"

The people of Tam Hung were inclined to keep problems to themselves as much as possible. Like small children in a school, they would nearly always stick together when local authority was on the scene. It would have been painful for anybody in the hamlet to bring a problem to somebody in the Popular Front forces, let alone the Vietnamese Special Forces people or the Americans.

The villagers' desire to keep their own affairs to themselves was in direct opposition to their desire for law and order on the night that Tran Cao Cha lost his mind.

Maybe the weather brought it on—there was the distinct possibility of heavy rain coming down from the puffy clouds overhead. More likely it was the combination of rain to come and heavy gunfire from the battle being fought near Duc Trang. And there was the maddening noise of all sorts of airplanes in the sky. When the whole business was over, one of the villagers who'd been mixed up in it said to somebody else that it was a little surprising that everybody in Tam Hung hadn't gone crazy a long time ago.

Tran Cao Cha was a toothless old man of fifty. He had lost his wife to Vietcong bullets and his son to the bullets of Ngo Dinh Diem's troops. His daughter had died in childbirth, and the child was dead too. His son-in-law, a nice, quiet lad, had been tortured and killed by the Cong. Tran had been living alone and getting by on handouts. Sometimes he would sit in front of his thatched hut and cry without making sounds. He didn't talk much. Everybody felt sorry for him, and he was considered a pretty nice old fellow until the night he went mad.

Nobody ever knew what pushed him over the edge, but a number of people in the village certainly felt the effects of it.

Ngo Doan Thanh had been the local government representative for six weeks when the incident happened. He wasn't considered a bad man, since he didn't steal or cheat any of the villagers. He was in his office in the only concrete building in Tam Hung. If he heard a stealthy sound near him, Ngo Doan Thanh would have turned swiftly and seen a toothless old man heading toward him. Light would probably catch the blade of the ax in his hands.

"Wh-what do you want?" the government representative might have said. His adam's-apple was as big as a young water buffalo and it would probably bob up and down in a frenzy while he tried to understand what was happening.

The crazy old man lifted his ax and brought it down against Ngo Doan Thanh's head, nearly splitting it in two. Some people swore later on that they'd heard a muffled *thock!* coming from the government representative's office.

Tran left the wooden building, ax still in his hand, and zigzagged over to the line of huts. He found Ho Boan Khah lying spreadeagled on his comfortable bed, mouth open, head back. At the sound of Tran's entrance, Khah must have come awake. He shouted something or other, then clenched his fists, jumped out of bed, and charged the crazy old man.

95

Tran took a step back, no more than that, so he could get the range, and then smashed the ax blade down across Khah's skull in such a way as to cleave it like an apple. Again and again the ax fell.

In spite of his madness old Tran must have known that Khah could very well have directed some attention on the hut because he had called out very soon after Tran came in. He left and went furtively over to Nai Ha's hut. Nai Ha was five years younger than Tran, but she was considered an old woman.

Nai Ha had been awakened by the shout, probably, and as soon as Tran hurried into the hut she tried to run past him. He simply raised the ax. A line of blood appeared across the old woman's scrawny breasts. Nai Ha buckled before she fell.

By this time, the blood on old Tran was soaking his few remaining hairs and pulling the clothes tight against his thin body. But he stumbled into the night and over to the next hut, where he found Co See, a married woman with two children, and the young widow named Ha Binh. Ha Binh had been living with the other woman for the last three days. She liked Co See and felt sure that Sergeant Ken Hubbard would approve of the change.

Ha Binh was awake when Tran opened the door of the hut she was sharing with Co See. She had been awakened by the shouting on the outside as people went back and forth and called to each other. She understood that something bad was happening but didn't have the slightest idea what it might be. Now, when she made out the blood-spattered old man with his ax in the darkened hut, she knew what had gone wrong.

"What do you want?" she asked.

He wouldn't talk; he only breathed heavily. But he wasn't moving forward either. All his efforts had tired him out.

"I have done nothing to you and neither has Co See," Ha Binh went on. "Isn't life hard enough without your doing this thing?"

The old man hesitated. That was when Co See awakened and looked from one to the other in the hut and realized that her children were on the same bed with her. At that minute Co See let out a scream.

The old man lunged forward, and the hut door suddenly opened on half a dozen men. They ran at the old one, knocking him to the ground and pulling the ax away from him. The attackers' bodies were blood-smeared, but they said nothing about it. Ha Binh, showing more presence of mind than anybody else in the small hut, was lighting a candle.

A man asked, "What shall we do with him?"

"Give him over to the Popular Front."

"I wouldn't want a dog in the hands of the Popular Front."

"You can't let him free with an ax in his hand."

"The soldiers are liable to arrest half the village for the murders if we don't turn him in."

Ha Binh said quietly, "Not necessarily."

"Quiet, widow! This is not a matter for you to discuss."

Co See said snappishly, "Anyone can discuss anything, in these times."

Ha Binh murmured, "The bodies can be buried and officers be told that the people are still in the village but not accessible at the time when supplies are being handed out."

"What about the Dai Dien?" The man who asked that was talking about the government representative. "His body must be accounted for."

"We can say that he was taken by the Cong."

"I think that is true, we can say so; but why involve ourselves in a web of lies?"

"For one thing the victims have food and blankets and cooking oil to be distributed among us," Ha Binh said quietly. "More supplies will be handed out before the absences are discovered, and those can be parceled out among us as well."

"True, but what about the old one here? He cannot be permitted to roam free with his ax."

"That's so," Ha Binh admitted, her face falling. "I don't know what to do about him."

One of the men grinned. "That is because you are a woman and cannot think ahead," he remarked. "I know the answer to that riddle."

"Well?"

"He only has to be confined to his hut. Let one of us be on guard for twenty-four hours a day, taking turns with others, of course. If he so much as sticks his head out the window he is to be killed. In that way, all will be well."

"And we continue this for as long as he lives? What happens when no more additional supplies can be obtained?"

"Then, and reluctantly, we turn him in to the authorities."

It needed some discussion before the plan was adopted, but the men agreed among themselves on the broad outlines of the plan and it was mainly a matter of deciding who was to keep watch and at what times.

Tran was told so clearly what was going to happen to him if he dared disobey orders that he understood. The blood was washed off him, and his clothes were destroyed before he was given others. He was led back to the hut he occupied and told again that he must stay there. Without the ax in his hands, old Tran didn't put up any resistance.

One by one the bodies were taken away and the blood traces removed from the huts and the wooden buildings. The bodies were buried secretly. Supplies that had belonged to the victims were parceled out among the conspirators, and the government representative's things alone were enough to make sure that Co See's children would be happy during the next few weeks.

The day-and-night guard in front of old Tran's hut got underway immediately. Nobody but the villagers who were involved knew what was happening. During the day village life went on as it generally did. Youngsters would run up to SF men, whether American or Vietnam-

98

ese, touch them, and run away, giggling. Women still sifted rice through fly-specked blankets. Other people cleaned eels in wicker baskets. Some people died of natural causes. The SF pacification program went on. Nobody else knew that a madman was being guarded in his hut by a number of secretive villagers who wanted nobody to get even the slightest idea what they were doing and why.

The guard of the moment, whoever it might be, would ask another guard to get the old man's food supplies for the week. The stuff would be left in front of Tran's door. The guard would knock six times, quickly. There would be a pause, and then the door would open and Tran would stick his head out the door, bend down and grab the food supplies, and close the door on himself for another week.

Ha Binh realized that the men who were watching over Tran were getting a profit from the experience that wasn't open to her. They were enjoying it. They might grumble among themselves or to their wives, but actually they knew they were doing something important, and that made their lives worthwhile. Ha Binh realized that she, too, wanted to find such an interest in life, wanted her life to be worthwhile and not useless. It was only a matter of finding an outlet for herself and her energies.

The conspirators were genuinely sorry when no more supplies for the missing people were being received. It was time to go to the new Dai Dien and tell him that old Tran had lost his mind. They couldn't keep up the watch over him forever.

One of the conspirators did suggest it, out of respect for the aged, but was turned down. A delegation of conspirators went to the new Dai Dien and told their story. He sent two soldiers to put Tran under restraint, having been told only that the old man had lost his senses and not that he had taken an ax to several villagers and his own predecessor. If he had known the truth he would've ordered the old man strung up from the nearest banyan tree.

The two Popular Front men opened Tran's door and found him lying in bed, his eyes open but not seeing anything. He was dead.

The contents of the hut were taken by the soldiers and given to the Dai Dien, who would hand them out to some of the more needy villagers. The conspirators were sore at themselves and each other for not having considered that a fellow of Tran's age might very well have died from natural causes; somebody should have looked into the hut before going to see the Dai Dien.

The argument lasted for a week and gave the conspirators something to talk about, but then they went back to the lives they had been leading before Tran lost his mind. They would raise pigs and tend the water buffaloes and the chickens and fix up bullock carts to help them get around from one place to another. But work took little time, and the men usually joined others in front of the granary, sitting around and chewing betel nuts and staring into space. There wasn't much for them to do nowadays.

Evelyn Colbert got back to her hotel and went to her room as fast as she could. She was still shuddering over what had happened in the house of that boy Dek Ho and his vicious father. She had spent a dreadful night, a ghastly night.

She hadn't meant it to happen, certainly not with a man whose name she'd never know and to whom she wasn't anything but a squirming mass on a bed, human material to be used and exploited.

Never again would she be able to make love with a man without feeling that she was dirty all over. Once she decided on that, it took no extra time for her to realize what she'd have to do. In a little while, a few days or a week at the most, she'd be seeing her husband again. When that happened she couldn't go to bed with him. In fact, she'd be letting him in for a certain amount of pain by what she was going to ask from him at a time when he was away from home and at war; but to Evelyn Colbert in her state of nerves there was nothing else to do. She had thought of the alternatives, but they didn't cut any ice with her. She knew exactly what needed to be done as well as knowing why.

She was going to ask Matt Colbert to give her a divorce.

Ten

THE GROUND was shaking all the time, partly on account of the air strikes and the blowing up of grass and tree stumps so as to make a landing zone for the big choppers. It was getting darker, and if the rains started, they wouldn't let up till doomsday.

This was going to be over in a short time if they could get out, Captain Matt Colbert told himself. The battle would be a success for the Special Forces—if most of the group lived to talk about it and didn't drown.

Choppers were starting to come in and pick up groups of Viet soldiers who were standing alertly as they could after more than two days of hard fighting. When a burst of gunfire started from a ridge, Corporal Overby quieted the snipers down by throwing a grenade.

"Better than a lullaby," Dave Lawlor said.

He was talking to a pal of his, Tom Dearden, who was the A team's second communications sergeant. He was a small guy for SF, with a face like a cornered rat. To Lawlor, who asked any man to be a good fighter and not much more, Dearden's face showed character.

"It ought to be okay now," Tom Dearden agreed.

Matt Colbert shouted, "Every available man on watch!"

Dearden and Lawlor turned to look into the distance, where sniper fire had come from. A wounded Vietnamese, waiting for evacuation, pulled off his wounded-in-action tag and reached for a gun.

It took more time to evacuate, Matt Colbert thought in a flash of despair, than the whole battle had taken. But the job got done carefully and with the help of a number of men who deserved rest as much as anybody.

The first raindrops came down as heavily as bullets that would dissolve on contact.

The choppers were coming in and scooting away with their cargoes. It seemed as if the stolid Corporal Overby had stopped Charlie's last threat.

As Dearden, Lawlor, and Colbert were on their way to the last chopper, Dearden suddenly turned back to Overby, who was trailing behind. "Corporal, get that Viet flag for us, will you? I don't think our men would want to leave it in the dirt."

Overby nodded and stooped over. Matt Colbert called out, "Wait, Overby! You can't be sure it isn't—"

There was the sound of an explosion as threads under the flag triggered a dynamite charge. Overby was blown to pieces while three men watched helplessly.

Dave Lawlor drew a deep breath and whirled on the man who would never be his pal again. "You stupid bastard!"

"How was I supposed to know—?" Dearden started.

"Next time you want a flag, take a chance on your own life and pick it up. Don't take a chance on somebody else's."

"I didn't know what was going to happen."

"You should've known it *might* happen, though. Do you think this place is a football stadium?"

"I said I'm sorry." The look that came into Dearden's eyes reminded Lawlor of somebody trying to stick a knife in some other guy's back. "Besides, I can't see what you're so excited about. You and him had a royal ruckus not long ago."

"Shut up!" Lawlor shouted, more angry than he could remember ever having been in his life. "Shut your ass."

Matt Colbert said tiredly, "Quiet down, both of you. There's no help for it any more."

"Yes, sir," Lawlor said reluctantly. Dearden nodded.

Matt looked over at Dearden. "Sergeant, I think we're going to have a long talk about booby traps when we get back to base."

Dearden nodded again, but not with so much eagerness.

He noticed uneasily that Dave Lawlor was looking at his neck as if he'd like to measure it. With his hands.

Matt sighed as he settled down in the chopper. One more man had been lost, and there was going to be deadly hatred against Tom Dearden from now on. But the battle could be called a success. Well, in a war you had to measure one thing against the other and then decide what was right or wrong.

The last chopper got away from Duc Trang just forty minutes before the heavy rain started.

The rain made Matt Colbert's men suspend every job of pacification and patrol that they generally did. Most of them sat around in the orderly room hoping that the stuff would stop coming down before the day was over. Some of them played cards. One afternoon Sidney Wheeler, the colored medic, and Jerry Garfine got into a hassle about a third man who wasn't in the room.

"You know damn well it's my turn," Garfine snapped.

"Mine," Wheeler said firmly. He was a good-natured man, but he felt he could be pushed too far. "I haven't won his cigarettes in two weeks."

"Wait a minute. You know damn well that when Marty gets his cigarettes he plays us for 'em and one of us wins. Right? I haven't won in two weeks, and it's about time I did."

"You won last week, and if you keep it up even Marty will suspect something. Just because he doesn't smoke it doesn't mean he's a complete idiot."

"Marty trusts his friends."

"He won't, though, if you keep on winni——"

"Hold on."

The door opened on Sergeant Bland. He was a moon-faced, genial-looking fellow whose specialty was heavy weapons and instructing Viet soldiers on how to use them. He was a good teacher and was hoping he'd become a full-time instructor on the college level when he got back to civilian life, which was supposed to happen in a few months. He was on "short" time out here, and

104

while another man might have become edgy about the chances of making it back, Marty Bland's disposition hadn't changed at all. He was carrying a black box in a gingerly manner, hands on the upper and lower corners set at diagonals to each other.

"That's a hell of a way to carry that Goddamn thing," Wheeler said cheerfully, his spirits lighter, as they always got when he saw Marty Bland again.

Marty eased the box down on a table and put a forefinger to his lips. "Quiet men, please. Do you know what's in there?"

"Two tons of cigarettes," Garfine guessed. The box was eighteen by twenty-four, he guessed, and couldn't have carried more than a few cartons.

"This is a lot more important," Marty said. "Did you fellows ever hear of nerve gas?"

"Sure." Wheeler drew his head back, startled. "You sniff it and you're paralyzed."

"Right. There are two tubes of nerve gas in this box, and if Charlie attacks the base in force all I have to do is take one of the tubes and throw it at a nest of Charlies."

"If this stuff is so good," Wheeler demanded, "why doesn't the army issue it?"

"Because of the publicity we'd all get if we used gas," Marty said. "I got it from Dave Lawlor, and he got it from a guy in the States."

"Open the box and see how good it is," Wheeler said. "Try it on one of the pigs."

"No, I promised I wouldn't open the box unless we're actually under attack in force. You fellows wouldn't want me to break a promise, would you?"

"Christ, no," Wheeler said loudly. "Not a *promise*."

Marty hefted the box tenderly and carried it out of the room. Wheeler and Garfine hurried out to get hold of Dave Lawlor, whom they found reading a magazine.

"What are you trying to pull on Marty?" Garfine demanded.

"I gave him an empty box, that's all. If he thinks there's something inside it, well, he misunderstood me."

105

"And suppose he runs for the box sometime when we're under attack. What then?"

"It'll never happen. Once Charlie shows up around here, he'll be as busy as any of the rest of us."

Wheeler said hotly, "You ought to get your head handed to you."

"Not by the likes of you." Lawlor grinned. "If you want to tell Marty he didn't understand me too good, I can't stop you, but—"

"At least you've got some human feelings, Lawlor."

"Let me finish. I was going to say that I can't stop you, but I'll tell Marty how come he always loses his cigarette ration at cards."

Wheeler and Garfine looked at each other. "Marty would only give away the cigarettes because he doesn't smoke," Garfine said. "He knows it's a friendly game."

"Uh-huh, but he thinks you guys are better players than him. He don't realize you're both cheating him bald-headed."

Garfine and Wheeler knew when they'd been out-argued. They got away from Lawlor and didn't tell Marty what they knew.

Marty had to get rid of some of his possessions to make space for the black wooden box, which Wheeler and Garfine knew was empty. What hurt them most of all was to see the little winks and conspiratorial glances he and Dave Lawlor exchanged during the next few days.

Garfine was working over a solitaire game that looked none too promising, when Sid Wheeler came over to him and asked for a few minutes of private conversation.

"Marty came over to see me today," the medic said, "and he looks rotten."

"What do you mean?" Garfine was alarmed.

"His complexion is very white, and his hands are a little shaky. He's hardly able to walk like he ought to."

"Well, the rain is bugging up everybody."

"This thing is different."

"What's the story, then, Sid? Don't futz around."

"All right. Marty thinks he knows what's wrong with

106

him. He thinks there's a leak in at least one of the tubes of poison gas in the box under his bed and the stuff is seeping out and getting to him while he sleeps."

Jerry Garfine said promptly, "Tell him that the God-damn box is empty."

"You know I can't do that."

"He'll have a nervous breakdown on us."

"I've got an idea." Wheeler tapped his head. "Could we steal the box?"

"No, because Marty will worry like hell about some-body else getting the effects of the nerve gas."

"What'll we do then?"

"Talk to Lawlor. He's a son of a bitch, but he isn't an inhuman son of a bitch."

They hunted up Dave Lawlor again. The sergeant was surprised to hear that Marty was in bad shape, and he was sorry he had started the whole bit, but he didn't want Marty to know it was a gag and hurt the guy's feelings.

They were all talking together when Marty came in and told Lawlor what was wrong. Lawlor said it was just Marty's imagination working overtime, but in the cir-cumstances he'd be only too glad to get rid of the box. Marty said he didn't want to give Lawlor a hard time on account of having done him a favor in the first place.

Then Garfine had a great idea. "Look, why don't we play for it? You know, a card game. Loser gets to keep the box."

"Well, I'm sure to lose," Marty said, "and I'll be right back where I started."

"Marty," Garfine said impressively, "I've got a hunch that this is one time when you might be lucky."

"Do you guys really think so?" Marty asked as if he couldn't believe his ears. "After all, I've never won any-thing from you guys. Nothing at all."

"Every new deal is a new game," Lawlor said impres-sively, rubbing his hands together. "I might take a hand in this myself."

"God knows you're welcome."

They decided on a game of poker, and the cards were cut. Marty looked worried, though, and Wheeler made what turned out to be the mistake of asking him about it.

"I figure I'm sure to lose the first hand."

"We can play a practice hand."

"No, that wouldn't be the same thing. It wouldn't really be the first hand."

"All right, we'll play for a few cents."

Lawlor asked jovially, "Why not make it more interesting?"

"I haven't got much money," Wheeler said promptly. "I'm in the army, you know."

"I mean something else," Lawlor said. "You guys play for cigarettes as a rule, I know, but that isn't fair because Marty doesn't smoke. Why not play for some work details? You know, the big loser takes over the crap details for a while."

"Now wait a minute," Garfine said, half-standing up. "This could get out of hand."

"Don't worry." Lawlor grinned. "Let's play for clean-up details at night for a month. Big loser gets our details. Deal?"

"Deal," Marty said enthusiastically.

The one way to build up Marty's confidence was by making sure he didn't lose. He came out all right, thanks to Wheeler and Garfine. One of them had to take the loss on himself, and Wheeler landed it.

"You fellows have certainly given me more confidence than ever," Marty said, beaming.

Lawlor suggested, "How about another round to decide who'll do the morning clean-up jobs for a month?"

"I really don't think—" Garfine began quickly, imagining himself stuck with a month's details.

Lawlor said, "I think we ought to have one more round like it. For Marty's sake."

Wheeler and Garfine made up their minds to stick Lawlor with the morning details, but Lawlor was too shrewd a player to let himself get cheated. Garfine had to arrange matters so that he would lose big and get the morning duties himself.

Eventually they played for the empty box that Marty believed was filled with nerve gas. They were using matches for chips, and because of a mix-up it took a little while to see who was cleaned out quickest. It was Lawlor, this time. He sighed and agreed to take the box back.

Garfine happened to be talking to Marty a little while later when Lawlor came over and told them that he thought there really was some kind of a leak out of the box, and he had gone to the boondocks and buried the damn thing under six feet of earth. The rain, Lawlor said virtuously, hadn't stopped him worth a damn.

Garfine got together with Wheeler just before lights out and said to him, "You know what I just figured?"

"Uh-uh."

"We've been screwed, that's what."

"How do you mean?"

"The whole deal was rigged up so that we would be stuck with a month's extra details. Lawlor and Marty between them figured out the whole shmear."

"Marty? I don't believe it."

"Well, can you believe he'd go for that story about a nerve gas?"

"Sure, if somebody he likes was to tell it to him."

"Rats! Marty's the nicest guy in the world, but I guess he resented losing to us all the time and he worked out the song and dance with Lawlor."

"Uh-uh," the medic said. "I can't imagine him taking advantage of us for trying to do him what we thought was an important favor. We didn't try to put anything over on him during the card game, and he knows it. Take my word for it, Lawlor was in this alone. When the breaks came his way, he took 'em."

"I'm going to get some sleep," Garfine grumbled. "I think I'll leave a four-o'clock call with the switchboard operator."

Garfine had to change his mind about Marty Bland,

though, and he was glad to do it. Marty made a point of going over to him or Wheeler whenever it would have been his turn for a detail, and taking it over. Nobody else but Marty would have done it, and nobody else did.

When his cigarette rations had been handed out to him, Marty suggested the usual game of cards with Wheeler and Garfine, to dispose of the things.

"Not me," Garfine said, showing his work-roughened hands. "I get the shakes when I pick up cards."

"Me, too," Wheeler said, showing his own hands. "Besides, you were lucky last time and you might hit it good all over again."

Marty threw his head back and laughed. "You guys are scared of *me?*"

Garfine and his buddy had to go along with it. The two of them would probably be known from that time on as the card sharpies who never wanted a game with the lousiest player in the Special Forces.

The Tam Hung camp didn't get visitors very often, especially American visitors. When somebody did come around, it always made for an interesting few hours.

For instance, there was the sad-faced comic whose stage name was John Doe. He was supposed to be very funny as well as completely helpless when it came to meeting any problem or getting along with somebody else. That was his stage character, and he played it for everything it was worth.

He started his show for the A team by looking around at the twelve men and taking a long pause, then saying, "My audiences keep getting smaller. I guess you fellows heard about me after the last camp I went to. No matter how you look at it, though, twelve-to-one is better odds than I've had in a long time."

The odds weren't strictly accurate. He'd brought a pair of cute girls along with him, and he was guarded night and day by soldiers on special duty.

"My first job was so bad, I remember, that the manager couldn't stand to look at me," John Doe went on. "He pushed my pink slip under the door."

110

There wasn't anybody on the A team who hadn't seen John Doe in a nightclub or on television, and every man had a rough idea about the way he did his act. Certain lines of his had been popular for years, and he'd work them into the routine for extra laughs because they were so familiar. Sometimes in nightclubs he would be asked to do certain famous routines of his, the same way a kid will ask to hear a story that he already knows by heart.

"The reason I'm so white isn't that I'm scared, but because I wash my face with detergents," he said at another point. "I never use makeup because the stuff just rearranges my wrinkles. Actually I'm in pretty good condition for a guy my age. I get plenty of exercise every day when I'm in the States—tearing up my loser's tickets at the racetrack."

He was full of cute tricks. If he happened to say a word so that it came out the wrong way, he would make a gesture as if pushing both thumbs against his upper plate. Before he was going to get what he hoped would be a really big laugh, he would click his teeth as if to show that he was so helpless he was lucky when he talked straight.

"Actually this GI outfit looks too loud when I wear it," he said. "On me, even black looks too loud."

When there was some sniper fire from outside the base, John Doe sighed and said, "Anybody who wants to shoot me can't be all bad."

Most of the men laughed, but Marty Bland found himself squirming. He knew that John Doe was well off and took it for granted that everybody in show business who became famous was rich. It irritated him and hurt that a man like John Doe should obviously have such a bad opinion of himself.

John Doe was working on the theme of fear now. When the sniper fire got underway again, he made that motion of tamping an upper plate where it belonged and said that his teeth got the shakes when a car started, so in a place like this they would be like a plate of Mexican jumping beans.

111

"I only came out here to do social work among mosquitoes," he added. "They need another filling station."

When his own act was over, he introduced one of the girls. She wore an evening dress and the two of them talked on stage for a while, the girl saying she wouldn't go out with John Doe. The girl had all the funny lines, and nobody in the audience noticed or cared that John Doe knew exactly when to come in after the crest of a laugh.

But Marty Bland was upset by the whole business of a man who obviously had such a bad opinion of himself. He was the only A team man who didn't laugh at the show.

It was over in three-quarters of an hour, and John Doe and the girls bowed to the sort of applause that would have shaken the rafters if they had all been indoors.

The men thanked John Doe afterward. Seen close up, his sad face didn't have much life in it. Marty didn't think of it as being funny, but it seemed to him that the man must be desperately unhappy.

It occurred to him later on that it might be okay if he went over to John Doe in a little while and said that he couldn't see why anybody ought to be so sad and unhappy and call himself names, even if he made money at it. John Doe might jab at himself again with one of those remarks of his, but at least he'd understand that there were people who genuinely liked him. Of course, John Doe knew he was liked by some people, but he probably knew it in his head and not in his heart.

Marty had no trouble getting past the soldiers who stood twenty-five feet from the visitor's tent. It was in the afternoon, and he hesitated for just a minute before opening the flap of the tent, wishing there was some door he could knock on by way of a signal that he was outside.

It was a good thing he did hesitate. John Doe was talking in a voice that was louder than usual and not at all agreeable.

"Don't give me that crap, baby," he was saying. "If I didn't know I was going to get me a lttle action, do you think I'd have taken either of you girls out here with me?"

The girl to whom he was talking murmured something in the way of an answer.

"Hell, baby, you're getting twenty million bucks' worth of goodwill, and you can live off it for the rest of your career, which probably won't be too long, considering that you got nothing but boobies. You'll have thousands of fans after this trip. Hell, I worked World War Two, Korea, and now this Goddamn dump, and it's always been a good deal for me."

He was making the war areas sound like vaudeville circuits. Marty was slow to resent most things, but he found himself backing away from the tent. The voice carried, though, and he could hear John Doe talking.

"I know twelve guys is no kind of audience, baby, but you can't get thousands at every show. If you don't work the small spots, the army doesn't let you work the big ones where you can get plenty of exposure. The damn thing cancels out."

Again the girl said something.

"Yeh, I saw him," John Doe responded savagely. "That one stupid son of a bitch who kept sitting on his hands. If I ever see that guy again, I'll skin him alive. Okay, baby, enough of that. Come over here now and give Uncle John a break . . . don't worry, baby. If anybody interrupts us, I'll shove his armpits right down his throat and get those stupid GIs out there confined to barracks for a year."

Marty Bland went back to his job of teaching two dozen Jeh tribesmen how to use a mortar. He never mentioned the patch of conversation he'd heard, but it seemed to him that he'd been right in being sure John Doe genuinely hated himself. Probably he felt that way because he knew John Doe too well. As much as Marty hated to think badly about anybody, it seemed to him that it would be right to feel some sympathy for the guy's self-hate. He had the idea, too, that the minute or so he had spent in front of the visitor's tent ought to have given him a look into something important about human nature, but he hated to ask himself what it might be.

113

It was sure not to be anything nice, so Marty Bland wasn't much interested.

Dave Lawlor tangled, in a way, with the next visitor. It was one of those sessions that Dave wasn't likely to forget as long as he lived.

This visitor came out one afternoon, complete with a cameraman and somebody else to take care of the sound recording. The fellow in charge was a TV news commentator named Gar Sheppard. He was a tall, sunburned, muscular man who wore GI fatigues as if he had picked them up in a snappy store back in the States. He had started on TV as an announcer, become an actor for a while, and passed up a chance for a Broadway show when some big brain at a television network decided he had the looks of a newscaster.

Nothing had come out of that particular setup, but Gar Sheppard had set out to make himself a newscaster type. He had bought thick glasses and practiced for hours talking in a solemn but punchy way. An offer to become a newscaster came through just four months to the day after he started looking for such a job.

There was good money in sitting around a studio and reading news bulletins off a teleprompter while looking at the camera or seeming to look at it, but there was more money in working overseas. He was putting in his second "tour" of Vietnam.

"I understand there's been some heavy fighting in this area, Sergeant," he said to Lawlor while the two of them were climbing into a jeep.

"It's over now."

"When do you expect more?"

"Not for a while. Charlie hasn't got the men."

Gar Sheppard scowled at his cameraman. "It looks like I had some wrong information."

"Excuse me?" Lawlor asked.

"Not at all, Sergeant. It's just that I was led to believe you were an active team right now."

"Oh, we're active all right. I'll show you."

114

He drove Gar Sheppard and his helpers into Tam Hung and showed them the buildings that had recently been put up, some of the new methods that the locals had been taught and were using, the attempts at schooling some youngsters for the first time. Gar Sheppard frowned continuously.

"Are there any Vietcong in this village?" he asked.

"Not as far as we know."

"Do the Cong attack this village nights?"

"Sometimes, but they're always driven off."

"Do they lose a lot of men? Do we? Do the Viets?"

Lawlor resented the man's saying that Americans and Viets belonged in different categories, but when he answered he told the truth. "Four of five KIA in a big engagement."

The corners of Gar Sheppard's mouth were drawn down in disgust.

"I'm afraid we've been wasting our time," he said, adding, "and yours, of course."

Lawlor hesitated. "I don't want to tell you your own business; but don't you think the work we're doing is worth a few pictures? After all, we're helping these people put their lives together again, and that's a lot more important than all the killing."

"Do you really think so, Sergeant?"

Lawlor nodded slowly. He lived for fighting and ought to have been in Gar Sheppard's corner, but fighting was one thing and taking pictures of it was like something dirty by comparison.

"Well, you're obviously not connected with television," Sheppard said, smiling. "Have you got any idea what it costs getting this film to San Francisco and then to New York? Probably not. When we're able to transmit film on the war as it's happening so it can be seen live, the expenses will go ever higher. As a result, I don't send anything back unless it's colorful and good."

"Isn't this colorful?"

"I'll let you in on a trade secret, Sergeant," Gar Sheppard responded. "The film with the best chance to be

115

shown is film about battle action. What's more, with my picture shown introducing it and commenting at the end, I get an extra payment, and a pretty good one, whenever the film is put on. So it follows, Sergeant, like a math problem—no battle action, no film shown, not much money made. On the contrary, my bosses write down a red mark next to my name if I send along any dull film, and I don't stay on the job long."

"We should be getting into Montagnard country pretty soon," Lawlor said carefully. "The team, I mean, for a day or so. The friendship ceremonies are colorful. You know, they pour rice wine over your boots and slash a water buffalo to death in your honor. These people are blood brothers of the Jeh, who—"

Gar Sheppard winced. "If we show some animal getting killed, we'll get a billion protesting letters."

"But it's part of the war."

Sheppard shrugged.

"It might be worthwhile to show that some Viets are friendly to us, instead of having people back home think that we have to fight like hell against all the Viets North and South. It might do something against the other side's propaganda, the stuff that does get through on our TV."

Gar Sheppard looked bored, eyes half-closed, lips moving as if he had to force himself to stifle a yawn.

"It would only be a trickle against a flood, Sergeant," he said, "and not stuff that's worth wasting a day or so trying to get. For all I know, there may be a chance at some better footage in the meantime."

"In case there's a fresh battle, you mean?"

"I'm afraid so."

Lawlor wasn't used to giving in, so he made himself keep talking. "These Yards have had it pretty tough at the hands of Saigon governments, you know, and the local representatives. Their best lands were stolen from them in most cases, and province chiefs even ordered some of them to dress Western-style and refused to let them build their houses on stilts. They joined the Fulro movement and fought the North and South Viets as a third force.

116

Things have changed for them now, thanks to our help. The local government has promised to give them back their lands, give them a special flag and an armed force under Yard command. Their kids are able to go to school again and the older ones have gotten scholarships overseas."

"Yes, Sergeant, I know."

"The point is that we've done something for these people, and you ought to be showing a little of that to our home folks."

Sheppard did stifle a yawn this time. "Well, Sergeant, I'll certainly take it under advisement and cable the home office as a favor to you, but I know what they'll say. Even if I'm told to go ahead with it, chances are that the film won't find its way to—what's wrong, Sergeant?"

"Somebody calling me. Be with you in a minute."

Lawlor walked over to the village granary, not showing that he was in any hurry to get there. Jerry Garfine was standing some five feet from a knot of village elders. His face looked grim.

"What's up, Jerry?"

"We're okay out here, but the news in other places isn't so hot."

"For instance?"

"Charlie has started something big over at Ban Me Hang," Garfine said moodily. "A lot of theirs and some North Viet regulars, too. The news just came through."

"How does it look for our guys?"

"We'll hold 'em and take more casualties than we get, but we'll have plenty of ours, too."

"Damn!" Lawlor said softly, then added, "See you later, Jerry. And keep shut about this for a while—okay?"

"Sure, if you want me to."

He could see Sheppard's inquiring eyes on him long before he walked back to where the TV commentator was waiting. Sheppard had geen talking to his helpers, probably chewing out one of them for having brought him on a wild-goose chase. The other men still looked uncomfortable, but Sheppard's face reminded Lawlor of some civilian doctor back home explaining that fees were so high because his expenses had gone up.

"Is anything new, Sergeant?" Sheppard asked. "Is there any good news?"

Lawlor had been on the point of telling the man what he wanted to know, but Sheppard's using the word "good" was enough to change Dave Lawlor's mind for him.

"Why no," the team master sergeant said slowly. "There isn't a thing."

Sheppard looked surprised. "You and the other man looked so serious that I thought fighting had broken out somewhere."

"No, it's not that," Lawlor said slowly. "We're digging a well for the villagers, and there's going to be a little trouble getting it finished by the target date. There's a hell of a lot of silt, you see, and the springs have been polluted because the people don't know the difference between—"

"Yes, yes," Sheppard said quickly. "Well, Sergeant, if you'll take me and my merry men back to the base, we'll pick up from there and be on our way."

"Glad to help you out, Shep."

He had never called the TV man by his nickname before, though Sheppard had asked him to do it. Now, though, he couldn't pass up the chance. For the first time since getting to talk with the self-assured Sheppard, in fact, Lawlor's feelings toward the man were those of downright friendliness.

Matt Colbert's generally grim and weatherbeaten face was relaxed for a moment.

"Seven days," he said to the men on his team, holding up that many fingers. "Seven days' R and R in Saigon."

Wheeler, the medic, who had just come into the orderly room, gave a sober nod. "We can use it."

"We leave on Friday," Matt said, "and I want to make sure that the roof won't fall in when Quang's counterparts take over for a week. Any important projects have got to be either finished or damn close to it by then, or else there won't be any leave whatever. Is this clear, Sergeant Lawlor?"

"Yes, sir."

"If any extra help is needed, there'll be a pool of men set up to take care of that," Colbert said. "Anyone with no special projects is to report to Sergeant Lawlor, who'll give me the information. I'll make the assignments."

Nobody would have expected anything less from Matt Colbert than that he'd look out for his men, but the jobs had to get done all the same. The men on Colbert's A team went at the work as if every minute was going to be their last one on earth.

Wheeler, the medic, had already been speeding up his daily program of inspections and injections when needed, and now he organized daily classes to teach the natives how to use soap. His Viet counterpart watched how he worked but couldn't hide his contempt for villagers who didn't know the basics of keeping clean. The man's thinly veiled contempt for some of his own people always bothered Wheeler, but there wasn't a damned thing that the medic could do about it.

Lieutenant Chris Ablett and Ken Hubbard and their Viet counterparts worked frantically to finish the well-digging job, but even with the help of demo equipment it was likely to take three days at least. When Ablett brought the problem to Matt Colbert, the captain rolled up his sleeves and went out to join the men.

Marty Bland was showing Viet squads how to clean their weapons and showing heavy-weapons men how to handle their mortars for best effect. It was uphill work because the men seemed to think that once the weapons were in action, perfect results were sure to follow no matter how the stuff was handled. Marty was the only A team man who agreed to work with Tom Dearden, who had been getting the silent treatment from others since his actions had caused Corporal Overby to be killed.

Nobody talked to Dearden about anything that didn't involve work. Dearden, though he was a solitary type who saved his money and had a weakness for local souvenirs that could be sent home, was apparently getting worn down by the treatment. He talked to Matt Colbert about it.

"I'll get you a transfer, Sergeant," Matt said, not able to keep from showing his own coolness to the man.

"Will you keep it quiet about the reasons, sir?"

"You know I can't do that."

"Then I'll be on the shit list no matter where I get sent—begging the Captain's pardon for the language," Dearden said, a little wildly. "That's not fair."

"As long as you're on this team, I'll do the best for you that I possibly can," Matt Colbert said, stroking his prominent chin. "But not if it means holding out information from any other A team."

From that time on, Dearden became more and more unhappy. Marty Bland, who couldn't keep up a feud, talked to him when nobody else was looking, but not even Marty could keep Tom Dearden from being morose.

Three days before leave, Marty was scheduled for a patrol in which he and Wheeler would go with ten Viets to kill any Cong they came across. Marty explained that Dearden would have to handle at least two days' work for him.

Surprisingly, Dearden said, "You're over the hump, aren't you? Only four months to go?"

"Three and three-quarters, actually. Three months and twenty-three days."

"Look here, how would it be if I took over for you, Marty? You know, as a favor."

"What do you want for evens?"

Dearden said shrewdly, "Tell the other guys I'm doing you a favor. That's all."

"Oh." Marty nodded. "You hope they'll stop bugging you, is that it?"

"That's it, Marty." Dearden hesitated. "We're the only Yanks here, us guys on the A team, and if we get into any hang-ups among ourselves—well, you know what I mean. It's bad for everybody. If I do this one thing, maybe I can shut 'em up."

"Sure," Marty said soothingly. "Well, I'll pass the word around and we'll see what happens."

Marty did what he had promised, of course, but all that Dearden got out of it was a visit from a scowling Dave Lawlor. "What in hell is the idea of your wanting to go out on patrol instead of Marty Bland?"

"Marty is over the hump, so I figured I'd do him a favor."

"The one you're trying to help is Tom Dearden," Lawlor said. "Do you think you can buy back what you did to Overby?"

Dearden made fists but kept them at his sides and hit his thighs again and again. "If I don't do something like it, I won't be able to get a transfer that's worth a damn to me."

Lawlor nodded, looking with guarded approval at the anger in Tom Dearden's eyes. "Well, at least you're not sitting on your ass and taking what you get."

Dearden looked as if he'd been reprieved. "Then you won't stop me from doing this? You'll let it go through?"

"If Marty wants to owe you a favor, that's up to him." Lawlor hesitated. "You were expecting an easy patrol, but you might get shafted instead. More personnel and maybe a few real dust-ups with Charlie."

"I told you I'll go."

"That's it, then."

Dearden waited, but Lawlor turned away. Dearden called after him, "Aren't you even going to wish me luck?"

But Lawlor wouldn't talk to him when it wasn't strictly necessary, and his own words stayed in Tom Dearden's ears.

The patrol was supposed to be made up of eighty CIDG men along with Dearden and Wheeler. The medic, his skin complexion almost the same as the darker CIDGs', walked over to the start of the big line to take the point-man position.

Dearden, seeing him, snapped, "Go back and let somebody else do it."

Wheeler looked straight at Dearden but didn't say a word to him and didn't move.

Dearden said, "If I get in any trouble I want to know there's a U.S. medic to take care of me—and so do the other men. You'll be a lot more handy if you're back in the line."

Wheeler said, "If I go back now and let one of them take the point-man job, they're going to start thinking I figure that any one of them is expendable but I'm not."

"I'll take the point-man spot myself."

Wheeler nodded, and Dearden went to the head of the line, each man fifteen feet apart. He had done the job before, and he worked with his rifle at the ready and eyes alert for traps. He had been in this country for the best part of a year on his last hitch, so he knew the jungle pretty well. He was able to budget for the risks, as much as possible on a job like being point man.

Nothing went wrong as Dearden led the patrol deep into jungle territory. There was no sign of Charlie, but the patrol did find one of his tunnels. The men destroyed rice and medical supplies because the stuff couldn't possibly be taken along, and acquired documents and war maps that might come in useful. At the end of the tunnel raid they destroyed the tunnel. Dearden, with some demo experience, had no trouble getting the job done.

At the suggestion of Dearden's counterpart, the men stationed themselves around the tunnel or close to it and waited for Charlie. The ambush worked out pretty well, costing Charlie fourteen men dead and twenty wounded, while another twenty managed to get away.

The point man was leading the way back to base as carefully as he had done everything else on this patrol, when the second man shouted something at him. Dearden instantly turned and cupped an ear to indicate that he hadn't made out the second man's words. The second man started to run toward him. Dearden gestured the man to take it slow, but it was useless. As the man came closer Dearden saw that less than three feet in front of him was the telltale glitter of a nylon trip wire, the sure cue of a trap that Charlie had set up.

The man was pointing down at the trip wire and shouting, "Snake! Snake!"

He raised a foot to stamp on it. Dearden knew he had been lucky to miss any sign of the damn thing while walking straight ahead, but he didn't want this CIDG man to get shafted, especially not while he thought he was trying to help all of them. Dearden pulled out both hands to stop him short, but did it so violently that he lost his balance and fell, landing directly on the trip wire. From the earth, a bed of iron spikes came up toward him.

Sid Wheeler rushed to his team member but had only to take one look at what was left of Tom Dearden. Then he winced, turned away, and walked back to his place in the middle of the patrol.

As soon as he was back at the base camp, he made a point of telling the others how Dearden had died. It was Dave Lawlor, as usual, not giving an inch, who said exactly what he felt and in such a way that everybody who could hear him was forced to agree.

"Dearden died like a man," Lawlor said, "but he was a son of a bitch for putting Overby in danger."

From the minute that Matt Colbert had announced a seven-day leave for the men, Sergeant Ken Hubbard had let one simple idea grow in his mind. *I want to take Ha Binh with me.*

He talked to her about it quietly one evening in front of the hut she shared with Co See. Children played noisily at one side of the hut, tossing wooden chunks that looked almost like joss sticks. As soon as Ken said what was on his mind, Ha Binh's heart-shaped face glowed with lively curiosity.

"Would you be permitted to bring a guest?" she asked.

"I'll do as much about that as I possibly can," he promised. "The point is simply whether you'd like to go. That's the first thing for us to get straight."

"It would be a great honor to go with you."

"In that case you'll go," he said flatly. "I'll see to it."

Ha Binh looked quizzically at the rawboned young man who was sitting at her side, fists tight and eyes half-shut in determination. Was he so young in experience that he didn't know his army people wanted him to have nothing to do with a native of the country?

Apparently he was. Ken Hubbard nodded and said again, "I'll see to it."

Not till next morning, when he hesitated in front of the wooden CP back at the base, did Ken realize that he had taken on a bigger job than he or anybody else in Special Forces would probably be able to manage. Matt Colbert was a good and even a thoughtful captain, but he was part of the establishment, and you couldn't finagle him into doing the sort of thing that the Pentagon looked crooked at.

Ken was young enough to try, though, so he walked in. Matt Colbert was pacing the room, his generally probing eyes resting when he stopped on the framed picture on his desk. In a little while he'd be out helping Ablett and Ken with the well-digging job in the village, but Ken didn't know that.

"Well, Sergeant?" Matt asked, stopping cold. "Is anything wrong?"

Ken told Matt Colbert what favor he had come to ask, talking carefully and dotting the Is and crossing the Ts.

"And you want me to let you take this girl along to Saigon? Is that the pitch?"

"Yes, sir."

"Will you give me a straight answer to one question?"

"I'll try, sir."

"Do you want to marry this girl?" Matt Colbert raised one sun-browned hand to keep Ken from answering too quickly. "I'm not suggesting that you should, Sergeant, but only asking whether you think you could."

"I don't know, sir," Ken admitted. "That's the best answer I can give."

"And too damned dangerous as it is," Matt said calmly. His jaw jutted out, the way it did when he was getting ready to pull rank on somebody. "Let me clue you in on something, Sergeant. If you permit this affair to go so far that you want to get married you'll be letting the girl in for security checks that will make anything you've ever gone through yourself look like a picnic by comparison. There's a long wait. There's a complete medical exam that the girl has to go through."

Ken flushed at the idea and its implications.

"I haven't finished yet, Sergeant. After the wedding, assuming it comes off, the two of you will have a few weeks together, and then the girl has to leave the country for as long as you're here. Are you getting my message, Hubbard?"

Ken nodded. Now that he remembered it, the ground rules for marriage had been talked about by the men at some time or other. The rules hadn't registered too clearly with him before.

"Now, Sergeant, I hope you understand that I'm not trying to hammer you down if you think that the girl is the only one for you and the odds are strong that you'll be happy. I'm a happily married man myself, and I'm looking forward to seeing my Evelyn when I get to Saigon."

"I'm very pleased for you, sir."

"Thank you, Hubbard. On the other hand, marriage to a local isn't a good idea by and large. There's a whole life ahead of you after Vietnam, and if you're going to work for other people instead of being self-employed, then a wife who isn't your color and your religion is pretty much of a handicap. I know what you're thinking, Sergeant; we've all heard that stuff about brotherhood and all persons being equal, and so on, and everybody agrees with it and says it's logical, but nobody lives by it in the real world. I shit you not, Hubbard. That's the way it is. That's what's *really* happening, baby!"

"Sir, all I came in here to ask—"

125

"I know what you came in for, Hubbard, and I'm trying to save you some possible difficulty in the future. I can't keep you from seeing the girl, but I'd suggest you make it perfectly clear to her that marriage isn't in the cards. And if you give her the reasons I've given you, it won't upset her a damn bit."

"Yes, sir."

"Now that I've talked my lungs out, Hubbard, do you still want to take her with you for a week's R and R?"

"Very much so, sir."

Matt Colbert sighed. "Do you know when a man realizes he has grown up? Not when he puts on his first pair of long pants or when he shaves or even when he sees people dying on all sides of him in a battle. It's when he realizes that other human beings are letting themselves in for a hard time and he has to stand aside and can't do anything to help. Hubbard, you're likely to have a rough time on account of this girl, and I can't do anything to stop it from happening."

Ken waited.

"Don't be too hopeful, Sergeant, but I'll make a try at getting her away. I don't know just how it'll be managed, but I'll try."

"Thanks very much, sir."

"You're rubbing salt in the wound, Hubbard. Now get the hell out of here."

"Have you heard the poop on Ken Hubbard and his local piece?" Jerry Garfine asked.

Sid Wheeler, the medic, shook his head. "I see no evil and hear no evil, dammit!"

"You're just a big, innocent country boy from way out in the sticks in Chicago. I know, I know. Well, Ken wanted to get this broad on the plane with him for seven sweet days of R an R: rolling and romping."

"Well, it would save him having to pick up the local stuff up there."

"That's what I figured, too. So he went to the old man for a clearance. Matt gives him a lecture on not taking the

126

local broads seriously and then says he'll do the best he can."

"So?"

"He made one or two tries through channels and he got *bupkiss* for his troubles. You know what *bupkiss* are, pal, or do you?"

"It doesn't sound like a local word, somehow," Wheeler said, grinning.

"You're right. Ken is up the well-known creek without the well-known paddle. He's stuck on the broad, and Matt hates to turn down his guys on any request that's even remotely reasonable."

"Wanting to live it up with your girlfriend is reasonable," Wheeler said. He shrugged. "It'll work out."

Garfine was irritated. "You take a real fine Oriental attitude to somebody else's problems, Sid."

"If he's got to have some local broad and won't take anybody else, that's Ken's hang-up and let him sweat over it." Wheeler folded his arms, kept his face rigid, and bowed partway from the waist. "*I* have spoken."

Matt Colbert had arranged a hitch for his men on an armed chopper that would take them to the Tan Son Nhut airport in Saigon. The chopper waited for them, and the men came on board slowly. Matt Colbert was last. His face was drawn, and his hands moved restlessly. The men who weren't married supposed that their captain was gung-ho because he wanted to spend time with his wife. Even a captain could get horny.

"Not yet," the captain told the chopper pilot and co-pilot. "One more passenger to go."

"I've already put eleven men and my two WGs on," the pilot said, gesturing back toward the waist gunners. "Who else is there?"

"A hospital case."

The men groaned. They didn't want to spend time that was part of their leave listening to somebody who had bought trouble sighing and moaning.

Matt Colbert looked severely at the men. "There's a

war going on, even at the capital, and this patient needs care. I've had hell's own time getting permissions for it, and there's no help for this, and it's got to be done."

Nine of the A team members muttered softly to themselves. Ken Hubbard, sitting far back in the chopper and with eyes closed, couldn't have cared less.

Sid Wheeler put in, frowning, "I don't know anything about a case so desperate it can only be handled in Saigon, sir."

"You're not the only medic on the reservation, Sergeant. It won't be long. There are one or two formalities, and then it'll all be over."

The men subsided. Garfine drew out a pack of cards and shuffled them absently. Dave Lawlor pulled out his transistor radio and tried to get some music from the armed-forces station, but gave it up and sat back and pushed himself forward as if to make sure he stayed in fighting trim. Marty Bland was reading *Playboy*, having obligingly torn out all the best pictures and given them to the men who asked first.

Matt looked behind him and then said, "Here we are."

Lawlor, scowling out front, saw somebody with facial bandages that covered everything but eyes and nostrils, and then he saw by the clothes that it was a woman. A suspicion leaped to his mind, and he looked admiringly at Colbert as the captain went to greet the patient and say a few words to the Viet medic who had brought her over.

"Well I'll be a seven-headed son of a bitch," Lawlor murmured. He whirled around. "Hubbard, get off your can and bring the girl in here."

Ken Hubbard's eyes opened wide. He looked out, then jumped up so quickly that he lost his balance. He was out of the chopper and hurrying toward Ha Binh in six seconds flat.

"The young lady is very sick," Matt Colbert told him. "I had to move heaven and earth to get her on the plane."

"Thank you, Captain. Thanks very much."

He helped Ha Binh into the chopper. When she was sitting down, he took her bandages off. The chopper got underway before he was finished with that chore. During the trip, he sat holding hands with Ha Binh. The other men on the A team didn't look once in their direction.

PART THREE

Eleven

A GOOD TOWN for R and R has got to have bars and brothels. Everything else is connected with one or the other. For instance, transportation gets you to the bar or brothel that you want to go to. Beggars know where to find good bars or brothels; at least some of them do. Money has to be changed over into local currency, because without it you can't get a woman or a drink, let alone getting both. Girls cluster around gambling joints so that such places are good for picking them up, but the gambling itself is pretty much incidental. A town could have all the tourist sights of the world rolled up into one, but without good bars and brothels it won't get the R and R business. Instead of the usual R and R, a leave ought to be called B and B. But a name like that one would be honest; and who the hell wants to be honest about liquor and sex?

The dancer stretched out a hand, letting her supple body move slowly, easily, languidly. She was gesturing in the direction of one man at the table in the northwest corner of the nightclub room. She pointed a finger at him, then smiled softly in his direction and gestured toward herself. And all the time she was dancing, her body moving rhythmically to the musical patterns set by the small orchestra behind her.

Dave Lawlor finished his shot glass just as the dancer paused in front of the gleaming beadwork curtains before taking her last bow. There was a hard smile of anticipation on the sergeant's face.

"I guess I'm elected," he said, smiling at Wheeler and Garfine. "Too bad for you guys. Go out and find your own action and leave me to mine."

"Hold it," Garfine said. "How do you know she was pointing at you?"

"She damn well was, that's how I know."

Garfine looked sullen. "I thought you had a girl in this town, an American girl."

"I do, but she's working." Lawlor didn't want to tell these two that he hadn't been able to talk to Nina Field because she was so hard at work on a wave of emergency cases.

Wheeler said, "This girl over here, the dancer, couldn't see you on account of the spotlight on her while she danced. You're invisible to somebody in a spotlight."

"Then she picked me out beforehand, buddy, but I'm the one who got the old come-on. And if I'm not coming right now, believe me I'm breathing real hard."

Decisive steps took Lawlor out the main entrance of the Club San Lo and around the corner to the rear. His self-assurance made the startled doorman give him the location of the dancer's dressing room. The door was partly open, Lawlor saw when he reached it. He grinned and rubbed his hard hands together.

He knocked three times on the door and was answered by a soft, controlled word of invitation. "Enter."

The dancer's face was flushed with satisfaction and pleasure as Dave Lawlor lumbered inside. If not for the brownish pigmentation of her skin, she could have passed for a Russian girl, he thought.

"Your performance was excellent," he said in perfect Viet.

"You are kind to say so." She curtsied. "I am named Mai Chi."

Lawlor gave his name and said, "I have hoped for the honor of escorting you to dinner."

"That would make me most happy," Mai Chi said, her eyes modestly downcast. "I know that a soldier has far too little time for introductions. Please wait while I dress."

Mai Chi walked around back of a small, bright screen. Sections of her dancing costume appeared on top of the screen's wooden rim. When she could be seen again she

131

was wearing black, and she wore it well. Her body was in every way a dancer's, long, smooth, and obviously supple.

Demurely she waited to hear his approval of the costume. Lawlor looked her up and down consideringly, then gave a solemn nod. He did approve. From the first second he had realized how fine she looked and how much he wanted her. Of course, he liked to feel that he had to struggle to get anything worthwhile, but he'd make an exception in Mai Chi's case. This was wartime after all, as she had said, and certain things had to be taken for granted.

Mai Chi insisted on returning to the club's front so she could have a few words with the manager. She put the whole thing politely, but Lawlor understood she was going to have her way about that. It was the first clash of wills between them, but Lawlor didn't make an issue out of it. She promised she would leave with him in five minutes whether she found the man or not, and then her eyes looked as if she was sorry for compromising even slightly.

They walked around the corner of the building that seemed as if it had been constructed with paper. Inside the club, while Mai Chi talked with a small, fierce-appearing man who glanced from her to Lawlor and back again, Lawlor looked around. He was cataloging the charms of Mai Chi for the third time when Garfine and Wheeler came up to him.

"Why aren't you guys dancing with some chicks?" Lawlor asked. "Or with each other, if you want that."

Wheeler brushed it aside. "Listen, Dave, this girl and that guy over there are setting up an ambush for you."

"How do you know?"

"I made a point of walking close to them, and I could hear a few words. She was saying she'll see to it that you're at Hei Do Street in an hour."

"Is that right?" Lawlor grinned. "We really *are* in for a tussle, me and her."

"Don't you care?"

"As long as I get laid, pal, and it's a girl who's good in

132

the hay, I wouldn't care if it turns out she poisoned her old lady."

"Be serious, Dave. Most of the entertainers in this town have got VC connections, just like most of the joints are really VC–owned. Everybody knows it and nobody does a thing about it. But this girl and her playmates are going to finish you off for real, I tell you."

"Don't worry, fellows. Oh, here she is."

Lawlor left with Mai Chi, not bothering to introduce her to his buddies. At the door he turned back for a sarcastic goodbye, expecting that the two men's eyes would be following Mai Chi's figure as she walked, but Wheeler and Garfine were deep in conversation, instead. Lawlor shrugged. Well, everybody could play the game his own damn way as far as Master Sergeant D. Lawlor was concerned.

He had rented a Chevy for his week's leave, and he opened the door for Mai Chi.

"I will take you to a very fine place," he said confidently. "A place to have dinner in."

"Not too long a dinner, I hope," she murmured. "I am not hungry, myself. Not too hungry."

Just hungry enough to give her playmates time to reach the address on Hei Do Street where he was supposed to be ambushed, Lawlor supposed.

He drove carefully through the dirty honeycomb of a city that would always be foreign territory to him no matter how many R and Rs he spent here. Mai Chi was giving a perfect imitation of a girl who wanted to jump into bed with him. Lawlor had developed a sharp eye for women, Viet and other kinds. It didn't often take him more than one good look before he knew which ones would, which ones did, and which ones were only playing games.

Just as he made a turn on two wheels, Mai Chi leaned forward and said, "I think we are being followed."

Lawlor hadn't expected an ambush so soon. He looked in the rear-view mirror and saw a driver and two soldiers in a rickety taxi. As the cab drove toward one area that a big neon sign almost reached, Lawlor could see Wheeler and Garfine. He swore. The two of them were trying to protect a guy who needed them and their protection like he needed a broken leg.

Lawlor smiled into the darkness and said, "The first order of business is to duck them. Hold on to your hat."

The job took him about five minutes longer than he had expected, but as soon as he knew he was being followed it was only a matter of time before he gave them the slip. It hardly made any difference that he was a pretty good man back of the wheel.

Mai Chi shuddered and said, "I don't feel safe."

"Nothing's happened to you so far, has it?"

"There is only one place where I really feel safe, and that is at my home."

So she was taking advantage of Wheeler and Garfine's foolishness to make a faster timetable for getting rid of him! Lawlor chuckled.

"I'll take you some different place," he said. "Just as safe."

"I must change my dress," she murmured. "I would feel uncomfortable in these clothes."

"If you just change and then we go out and eat someplace else, fine."

"I promise."

Yes, it was going to be a damn interesting session!

Mai Chi's address was in Hei Do Street, of course, in the northeast part of town. She made believe she was lost and delayed them for some twenty minutes. Then she decided she knew where she lived and led him there.

Her home was a small one-story affair, quiet and very flimsy-looking. It stood alone on a block, and it would have been possible to slaughter a hundred men without anybody in the next house hearing it. The nightly harassment and interdiction firing had started up while Lawlor was in the middle of his drive, and he cursed it quietly under his breath. It reminded him too much of other places where it was even harder to get a woman.

Mai Chi waited when they stopped, not opening the

door herself. Lawlor was tempted to let her wait, but he shrugged instead and got out of the car and walked around the front of it. Then he opened the door for her.

"Come inside and be at ease while I change," Mai Chi offered.

"I'd rather wait out here."

Worry lines appeared on her face, but she made a gesture back of her as if to pull the dress more tightly around her body and stepped out of the car in one fluid motion. She hurried toward the house.

Lawlor slid into the car and decided he'd wait. No doubt she'd come back again. If she and her VC playmates wanted to ambush him they'd have to pick a spot where the odds were in Lawlor's favor. Before they could even come close to reaming him, he was going to get Mai Chi in the sack.

A window opened in the house, and Mai Chi was looking out. "Please come in," she said. "I need help with something."

"Come out here and I'll fix it if you really need me."

"In that case, then," she said, and he could see her stiffening. "I wish you good night."

She closed the window on herself.

Lawlor's lips thinned. He decided on taking a cruise around the block and then coming back. She'd probably change her attitude and let her friends follow them someplace else, which he didn't mind as long as he and Mai Chi were going to be alone for a while.

The ignition key was gone.

Lawlor realized what had happened. The conniving little bitch had made believe she was pulling the dress more tightly around her, but in the darkness she had snatched the ignition key, and he'd have to go inside the house to get it back.

He almost wished that Garfine and Wheeler, those numbskulls, were with him. Together they'd be a match for any hoods the VC could throw at them.

A match . . .

135

Dave Lawlor looked to his right at the flimsy little house and smiled for the first time since getting here. He stepped out of the car and hurried along the pathway as if he was about to go straight into the house, but swerved and crouched when he was near one of the windows.

He pulled out a pack of matches from a pocket and lit one noisily, but doused it by holding it between closed hands in such a way that it was starved of air.

A man's voice could be heard inside the house, but Lawlor couldn't make out what he was saying. Mai Chi answered quietly.

Lawlor slipped the cellophane from a pack of cigarettes and started crinkling it quietly but with rising intensity. He gave a loud laugh, still crackling the cellophane between his hands, and walked in such a way that his first noisy steps were followed by quieter ones.

As he had expected there was a babble of noise inside the house as Mai Chi spoke and one man responded and then another. Three different people were talking. There weren't more than two men in the house.

The odds against him were small enough so that he could handle whatever came up. When he had taken care of the two hoods, he would drag the girl into the bedroom and take real good care of her.

What was more, nobody would be able to say it had been too easy for him to get this chick into bed. He had never liked things to be too easy.

There was a darkened window at one side of the house, and it was open from the bottom. Lawlor eased it open so that it could let him through.

Marty Bland stood in front of a building that looked spotless from outside. Every flame-red brick seemed to have been washed only a few minutes ago, and the four square windows facing this street gleamed in the late-October sunlight. A black-and-yellow printed sign had been put in the exact center of an easel at the left of the narrow aisle.

A middle-aged Viet civilian was walking slowly along

136

the aisle. As he reached the other end of it, wheezing and sighing, he found himself stopped by a burly usher who had been standing behind a table.

"Raise your hands," the usher growled.

The middle-aged man did it as slowly as he had done everything else so far. The usher tapped his palms up and down the withered body with brisk and mechanical competence, then stepped back.

"Pass," he growled.

A younger man was on the way inside too, but this one looked belligerent when he realized he was going to be searched. A more careful look at the guard's heft made him change his mind. The guard found a pocket knife, which the young man said he used for cleaning his nails, and put it into a white envelope. He wrote something across its face with a soft pencil, then eased the tip of his tongue over its extended flap before sealing it. He put the envelope into a different drawer, closed it firmly enough to suit him, and then raised a bulky thumb in the direction of the black-draped door behind him.

"Pass," he growled again.

Marty was staring but whirled around when somebody tapped his shoulder. He turned to look at a fellow named George Hill and then at Hill's friend Cobbett. The two men were Regular Army, and Marty had run into them after a few hours in town. The truth was that he didn't particurlarly like either man, but they had latched on to him, and Marty couldn't bring himself to tell them to go fly a kite. He had agreed to meet them in front of this movie theater at four in the afternoon, and from there they'd all go to some party that Cobbett knew was going on.

"It must be a kick to be searched before going into a movie," Marty said lightly. "I'm almost tempted to go in myself."

"The hell with Doris Day pictures," Hill said. "We've got a party."

"I promised we'd buy the liquor," Cobbett said, "but I've run out of dough. You too, Hill?"

"Yeh."

Marty offered quietly, "I've got about a hundred p-notes with me."

Hill opened his mouth to say something but decided against it. He was a tall blond with hard eyes. Cobbett was dark and heavy-lidded, with thick lips always on the point of slobbering. Each man had made the army his career, and neither was able to say anything good about another branch of the service.

Cobbett said, "You've got plenty more'n that, I'll bet. You're probably crawling with dough."

Marty chuckled. "Whoever told you that is lying in his teeth."

"I seen you before and you don't spend nothing, pal. That means you've got it somewhere."

"It's home. I send most of it home."

"That's what all the tightwads say," Hill said. "I remember a guy we worked on once who—"

Cobbett put in promptly, "Knock it off."

"Okay, okay, but if we're going to get something to drink, let's do it now."

Marty looked up and down the street. Storefronts littered with papers and crushed cans led to places that were run by fortune tellers, dream interpreters, tea-leaf readers, root sellers, and charm sellers. There wasn't a food store in sight, let alone an outlet for buying liquor. At the corner, half a dozen middle-aged men stood and talked listlessly.

Marty ran a hand along his thinning hair. "I don't see any good stores."

"We'll find one," Hill said grimly.

They turned down a street that seemed empty by comparison with the place they had left. Their footsteps raised echoes. Cobbett glanced questioningly at Hill and then at the chipped asphalt, the blank storefronts, the antique houses.

The place they wanted was on one of the sidestreets that branched off it. Hill and Cobbett saw a car in front

138

of the store and looked admiringly at it. It was a Yank job with too much chrome, too many headlights, and more than enough seating room for an army transport plane.

"That car can probably go through traffic like a good football player down the field," Hill said.

Cobbett promptly forgot about the car. "Stick to business if you ever want wheels like that, George. Stick to business."

Marty looked puzzled but didn't make any comment. With each man carrying a bottle, they led the way to still another side street and a three-story house. Marty climbed stairs behind the other two. The door was opened by a slim fellow with no eyebrows, lips as thick as a pair of razor edges, and a nose that had been broken twice. He gave Cobbett and Hill an unpleasant smile, then turned to Marty.

"My name's Sam Drake," he said in almost a soprano voice, offering a hand that felt as if it had been carved out of hot cereal. "Come on in."

A rock 'n' roll tune was being brayed over the blue-and-white thumb-sized radio in the northeast corner. The tune finished with what sounded to Marty like flatulence.

"That idiot music is okay when you haven't got work to attend to," Sam Drake said, shutting off the radio with a flick of thumb and forefinger.

Marty cocked his head and asked, "Isn't anybody else here?"

"Follow me," Sam Drake said. At his left and in the kitchen was a mud-brown table with club soda, an ice bucket, and a dozen glasses.

"That's for tonight," Drake said, "when there'll be a real reason to celebrate. Or at least there'd better be."

"I don't get this." Marty had sensed something wrong. He drew back a step, noticing that Hill and Cobbett watched him out of hard and narrowed eyes.

"Me and my pals have got a foolproof idea for getting good money in this miserable town," Sam Drake said. "All

139

we do is find a soldier who claims he's putting dough away for other people, and we keep him here until he gives it to us instead. Simple, huh?"

"But I really haven't got—" Marty began.

"Let's suppose you're on seven days' leave," Sam Drake said. "I'm picking seven because it's the first number I can think of. You'll hold out for a day or two, but time is slipping past and you might never make it alive for another R and R. So you won't mind tramping the town in bare feet if you have to, as long as you get rid of us. We'll get the money."

"That's the straight poop," Hill said. He nodded at Drake as if there was a special agreement between them.

It was Cobbett, though, who answered the question on Marty's mind. "And when our own leaves are up, we donate you to the guys who take over after us and we'll split afterward, just in case you think you can wait longer than us."

"Get used to the idea," Hill rasped. "This is going to cost you some dough."

Marty shrugged. "You can search me and take whatever you find."

"That'll do for a start."

The only money he carried with him was sixty piasters, which was left after he had bought some liquor for what he had expected would be a party.

Cobbett glanced at the key that had been taken from Marty's pocket. He lifted it and said carefully, "It won't do any harm to search his place."

Marty looked irritated at the notion of strangers pawing around the few items of clothing he had taken with him. Drake and Hill saw the response. Cobbett chuckled.

"Pay dirt," he said. "I'll get it."

"See that you do," Drake snapped.

Marty asked, "Does anybody mind if I have a drink?"

"Help yourself," Hill said, grinning. "It'll be costing you plenty."

"I'm glad you guys aren't trying to cut up," Marty remarked.

"We never have to, like Sam said. When we get the money, you'll write out an IOU for that amount, so there won't be any question about us not getting dough we were entitled to. Oh, we've figured out everything, pal. You won't want to bitch to the MPs later on."

Marty made himself a Cape Codder and wondered how many other guys had been taken in by this unholy crew. He hated to get mad at anybody, but he was getting mad now.

Cobbett got back in three hours. There was spittle on the corners of his heavy lips, and his dark hair had been ruffled, probably by himself when he began to get sore on account of what he hadn't discovered in Marty's room.

"Nothing," Cobbett reported. "Not a Goddamn nickel! He sent me on a wild-goose chase, and I'm for taking it out of his Goddamn hide."

Drake turned around to see how Marty was reacting. Marty looked surprised, maybe at the idea that anybody would want to put a finger on him except maybe a North Vietnamese *bo doi*. He glanced reproachfully at Cobbett, as if blaming him for something but not wanting to say so.

Cobbett got angry. "What in hell are you looking at like that for?"

"I'm surprised to hear you saying—well, *you* know."

"I know?" Cobbett roared. "I don't know a Goddamn thing except that you haven't got a nickel to your Goddamn name. Any jerk who goes on leave with only a hundred p-notes, one dollar in real money, ought to—what the hell!"

Marty had winced again, like a spaniel being kicked.

"I get it," Drake said, whirling on Cobbett. "What did you do with his dough?"

"What dough? What in hell are you talking about?"

"With his money, that's what."

"Me? I didn't find any. I just got through telling you."

"Me and George over there, we heard what you said. That don't mean we believe a word of it."

141

"Christ on a crutch! If you don't believe me, go ahead and search me."

He stood with legs apart and arms stretched out as if he was doing an exercise.

"If you want to be searched it stands to reason you got rid of the dough already," Drake snapped. "You hid it."

"I didn't find nothing, I tell you."

Even George Hill, who wasn't the smartest of that three by any means, looked at Marty and saw him wince again.

"Don't you know what he's doing?" Cobbett demanded. "He's bluffing. He's trying to break us up and put us against each other."

"Maybe he is, but not on purpose. No stupid cluck would take a seven-day R and R with only a hundred p-notes. You know it and so do I. In that case, where's his money?"

"I searched that room till I was blue in the face, and he hasn't got a dime there. Not a dime."

"You're full of shit!" Hill snapped.

Drake said, "Give us your key, Cob, the key to your own room and we'll look it over. Maybe you dropped the dough off till you could get rid of it."

"Go ahead and look," Cobbett started furiously, then shook his head. "Just a Goddamn minute now. I've got my own money in the place, but there's no signature on it or anything. How do I know you two won't figure it's stuff I took from him instead?"

"Cob, you don't," Drake said levelly. "But if we aren't going to get the cluck's dough, you sure as hell won't be alive when you get away from here."

"I'm not handing over the key. If you want it, you'll have to work for it."

"That's a deal," Drake said. "Cover the door, George."

Drake took a whiskey bottle off the kitchen table and cracked it at the neck. Holding the short end so that the jagged glass pointed at Cobbett he moved toward the other man.

Marty couldn't have brought himself to look over at

142

the two men, even if he'd felt he had the time for it. He skirted them. Back of him he heard Cobbett call out as if he had been hurt, and then Drake drew in a deep breath. Probably Cobbett had been able to do Drake some harm in spite of Drake's carrying the jagged edge of a whiskey bottle.

George Hill was watching the two men in the same hypnotized way that a bird watches a snake. Marty, running around to reach him from the left, had only to give Hill a straight-hand punch against the left side of his neck, and George Hill went down without a sound. Marty was half-apologizing under his breath as he got the door unlocked. He would have opened it instantly, but he had to shove Hill out of the way, and in the time that took, Drake saw what was happening.

"Get him!" Drake called out, and lunged toward the door. "Come on, Cob!"

The other man gasped, knocked out of commission for a while at least. Drake lost enough time sizing up the situation so that Marty was able to open the door and get out.

He ran like hell. Back at the billet he approached the MPs and told them what had happened to him and where. He rode with a flock of them in hopes of tracking down the apartment location but couldn't find it in the maze of crooked little side streets. He had to give it up. The MPs told him to keep an eye out in case he ever ran across those crooks again.

Marty heard later that one of the soldiers, the guy who had given his name as Cobbett but whose real name was different, had gone to the U.S. Hospital to have a wound patched up. He said he had picked it up during a fight in some bar. MPs had alerted the hospital people to be on the lookout for a case like that one, and the GI was identified and arrested in a short time. The doctor who had made the connection between the man who'd called himself Cobbett and the warning notice, as Marty found out, was an attractive girl whose last name was Field.

143

That evening at the billet, Marty waylaid Lieutenant Chris Ablett and gestured him over into a corner.

"I'd like another hundred p's, lieutenant," Marty said.

"Another hundred?" Ablett grinned. "You're spending it like a drunken—uh, soldier."

Marty said, "You agreed to keep my spending money for me till I'd ask you for it, sir, so I'm asking you for another hundred in p-notes. If it's handy, of course."

"The money's yours in the first place," Ablett said reasonably. "Why shouldn't it be handy?"

"Thanks very much, sir."

"I figured you'd be about the number-one target for any smart-ass sharpster in Saigon, Marty, and if you haven't got much loot at any one time it's sure to keep you out of trouble. I've been right so far, haven't I?"

Marty swallowed hard, but he was a good-natured fellow and he hated to upset anybody's calculations. "Absolutely right, sir," he said fervently. "A hundred percent right."

For Ken and Ha Binh the first three days of his leave were fine. They had moved into a hotel and were living together. Ken found in Ha Binh one of those rare bed partners he knew he would always remember with affection. She was uninhibited but without the feeling of desperate gaiety that Ken had seen women take on in bed. Her attitude seemed to be, "We should do this thing which makes us happy."

What was almost as good was that Ha Binh didn't call herself names after a sexual episode or tell him in an agony of self-hatred that she'd been to bed with more men than she could count. He was used to that sort of thing, and to saying things that didn't mean much but turned out to be soothing. It never stopped surprising Ken that in spite of all the talk about sexual freedom a girl still behaved as if she were giving away the only valuable thing in her life. He guessed that married sex was better for a woman and worse for a man. Nothing could beat that feeling of illicit pleasure.

With Ha Binh, though, it was different. She kissed him

lightly on the top of the head when a night's sex play was finished, sighed gratefully, lay back in bed, and then went to sleep.

On his first night with her, Ken had a nightmare, and next thing he knew Ha Binh was comforting him, stroking his face while she murmured soothing words to him. On the second night he woke up because he wanted to use the bathroom and noticed for the first that Ha Binh slept facing him. He was touched by it and walked on tiptoes with enormous care.

When he came back, still softly, Ha Binh stirred and asked, "Where have you been, Nguyen Van Mieng?"

Ken said nothing. Her eyes opened wide and he could sense that she was staring directly at him in spite of the darkness. She sighed.

"For a moment I thought—"

"I know, dear. You thought I was your husband."

"Yes."

He was on the point of saying, "Maybe I will be, in a very little while." He had never felt such a rush of affection for another human being.

During the days he was finding out that the two of them agreed about important things. Ha Binh's experience of the world might have been physically limited, but she was shrewd and intuitive. She was curious about everything. She had heard that every American was rich and that Negroes and Indians were treated as badly as her own government had treated the Montagnards. She would listen intelligently to the things he told her and respond in such a way as to show that she had absorbed what she'd heard. Ha Binh, to add it up, was a strong, sensitive, shrewd, attractive, loving, and responsive woman, and Ken Hubbard figured he was going to marry her.

He decided to talk to her about it on the fourth day of his leave. He had been living in a hotel and hadn't seen an American soldier for a couple of days, so he was inclined to feel that there wouldn't be too much trouble persuading *them* to do what he and Ha Binh would almost certainly want.

145

He did talk to Ha Binh about her staying in Saigon, which was further removed from trouble than the little village where he had found her. Ha Binh looked scared by the notion, and she examined Saigon in a different way from when she'd first reached it, trying to decide how things would be if she turned into a small cog in what struck her as a very big machine.

"It is all so different," she said.

"Do something for me, Ha Binh. Keep an open mind about it. Don't decide right away."

"Very well."

In the late afternoon, when it was plain to him that Ha Binh was hungry, he picked out a restaurant for them. Although its window was boarded up, he led them to seats at the table closest to it and wasn't surprised when the waiter acted out of long-time habit and came over quickly to the showplace table to get their orders. Ha Binh went through her usual agonies in deciding what to eat. Ken ordered lightly, as he always did, and Ha Binh made a point of remarking about that.

"No wonder you are so thin," she said. "You eat nothing but feathers and air."

Ken said, "I'll have you know that I put on twenty-five pounds since I got into the outfit."

"Before the gain in weight, Ken, you must have been invisible."

They smiled at each other, feeling comfortable and relaxed. Ken was beginning to get some idea of what living would be like with somebody who knew him well and cared about him. Living might improve, he decided, with the likes of Ha Binh. And the two of them happened to have so many things in common . . .

He realized that some sort of disturbance was taking place outside. It was possible to see through the half-opened door.

A man flashed into Ken's sight at last, zigzagging across the street and nearly being run over by a car that screeched to an angry stop when it got past him. In his right hand he carried something that glinted metallically beneath the sun but was splotched with redness at the far end. Ken made it out quickly enough when it was lowered, and the identification started something in his stomach. It was a kitchen knife the man was carrying.

The man reached this side of the street and glanced back feverishly.

A United States Army man was running after him, a man whose pale skin was flushed with exertion. In one stretched-out hand he carried a stick raised so that it could be used as soon as he was in reach of his target.

The fugitive turned and ran blindly, desperately, into the restaurant. The eyes of every diner in the place followed him as he pounded the length of it, then swiftly opened one door and glanced inside and ran to another door.

The U.S. Army man, a sergeant, rushed inside now, yelling in English, "Stop, dammit, you son of a bitch! Stop!"

The fugitive slammed another door shut, then wheeled around and ran in a frenzy toward the entrance, wiping sweat out of his eyes and zigzagging in a way that brought him close to the table where Ken sat with Ha Binh. The closer he came, the more that red-tipped knife seemed to glint in his hand.

Ken glanced from the knife to Ha Binh, swiftly measuring the distance between them. It wasn't nearly as wide as he would have wanted. He got to his feet, making thick fists as he took a couple of steps to get in front of Ha Binh and closer to the oncoming fugitive.

The man advanced, wiping his eyes with a forearm to clear them of trickling sweat. His gasping breaths were like explosions in Ken's ears.

As the fugitive came closer, he swerved toward the entrance. He could have made it without getting closer to Ken and would have been able to scoot out of the place, but his balance wasn't too good by then and the swerve nearly brought him up against Ken. That was much too close. Ken's fist snaked out, finding softness under the hemp that the man wore instead of a belt. Then he stepped out of the reeling man's reach, gesturing Ha Binh to keep her place.

The fugitive doubled over, and a long breath came whickering out through his nose. A spider's web of spittle stretched out to the dark clothes he was wearing.

The Regular Army sergeant came up behind the fugitive and twisted one of his hands painfully against the man's thin back. He said grittily, "Goddamn murderer!"

The helpless man made a motion with the hand that was still gripping that red-stained kitchen knife. Ken forced the knife out of the slim hand by one swift judo chop that made the man call out with pain.

He heard a rumbling sound from a number of throats and turned around. More than a dozen diners were standing up, their faces taut with anger. One man had tucked a cloth napkin between the front of his collar and his betel-colored skin, but now he whipped it off and stood glowering at Ken and the sergeant.

"You let him alone," a woman squealed. "You stop hitting him—do you hear?"

The sergeant looked as if he wasn't able to make out one word of the language, but he did know the way to size up a crowd.

"I'm taking him to the nearest local cop," he said thinly in English. "God help the first one of you who tries to stop me."

He moved the prisoner toward the door. Somebody shouted in Vietnamese.

"Foreigner! Devil!"

The sergeant looked to his right, then suddenly whirled and shoved his prisoner full-strength against the partition next to the partly opened door. The prisoner landed against it with a moan. In the time it took him to crash against wood, the sergeant had stooped down lightly and picked up the stubby bloodstained kitchen knife and tucked it into a pocket. Before the prisoner could possibly have got his balance back, he was in the sergeant's iron grip again.

148

The sergeant said harshly, "Let's move!"

The crowd drew back, but somebody called, "I'm going, too."

Somebody else said, "We all saw the attack."

Ken turned to Ha Binh. "I'm going along with the sergeant."

Ha Binh reached out a hand to touch him softly. "Is it necessary?"

Her attitude surprised him, but he wouldn't show it. "Yes. My help may be needed."

"I'll come with you."

The four of them walked for a block and a half, and people behind them talked to others, who joined what was becoming a parade. There was a uniformed local policeman standing in front of a newsdealer display that looked so much like the Stateside product that Ken was startled. The uniformed man had been thumbing idly through a Hong Kong magazine, but when he saw the crowd he put the magazine on a wire rack strung parallel with the top of the newsstands, then eased it on to one of the wooden clothespins that were suspended from the wire.

He heard the army man's story and Ken's corroboration and translation. People in the crowd put in a few words every so often while Ken was talking. The uniformed man nodded grimly, then ordered the sergeant to let go of the fugitive. The sergeant did it slowly.

The policeman held the battered fugitive by a hand, almost as if he were dealing with a small boy. He walked with him to the glass double doors of a shabby gray building on the next block. When the people in the crowd looked as if they were going to follow inside, the policeman turned around and shouted at them to stay back. The people muttered but did it. Every face that Ken could see belonged to somebody who was sweating and mad. There must have been at least three dozen men and women along that block. Ken saw a child riding his father's shoulders to peer soberly at what was going on. Other people who lived close by were looking out the windows of their houses and calling to each other. Everybody within earshot seemed to have a different idea about what to do next.

"We'll all go in at the same time."

"No, we stay out here and wait."

And a new voice, deep and confident: "Friends!"

A wooden two-story house hugged the left side of the gray building, and a man had got up on the top step of that porch and raised himself on tiptoes. For the next minute or so he kept repeating the word "Friends."

The crowd turned to him at last, and that deep, rich speaking voice seemed to fill every cranny of the street as he demanded that the crowd take action without saying what he thought the action should be. Ken saw the man's eyes gleam maliciously and his lips twitch at the corners when he felt that the crowd was with him.

Ken threw his head back and put up both hands to be used as a megaphone. But he turned when he realized that Ha Binh's eyes were darting swiftly up and down his body.

"Don't speak now," she urged him. "You are a foreigner, and nothing you say will be well received."

He looked away from her and called out as clearly as he could, "Send five people inside as a committee to find out what is being done and why."

He repeated himself twice, and his throat felt as if he had swallowed sandpaper. The speaker gave a contemptuous glance in Ken's direction, but before he could say anything a uniformed policeman had come out of the gray building and was gesturing at Ken.

He nodded and walked up the stairs to the building entrance. Four or five men started to follow but were held back by the officer's glare.

Ken said loudly, "I want these people to come in with me and the others to do nothing until they hear a report from their friends."

His throat felt tortured. He saw people staring consideringly at him. Others were nodding and muttering their approval of what Ken had suggested. Ha Binh's face was

150

taut, he saw, and a strained grin briefly dyed her lips gray.

The police officer nodded finally, then gestured Ken and five Vietnamese men inside the building. There was a high-ceilinged anteroom where several uniformed men sat around and stared at the new arrivals. The officer led them down a long corridor to a middle-sized door. He opened that door and stood aside to let Ken and the others come in.

This was an office with three file cabinets in which some drawers were open, a big window that there probably wasn't time to keep clean, and official papers on a steel desk. The visitors' chairs were simple hardwood jobs. The ranking officer inclined his pudgy head as Ken and the other people walked in.

The Regular Army sergeant said, "This man saw it."

The ranking police officer had noticed Ken's green beret. He asked in Vietnamese, "Do you speak the language?"

"Ah." The bright blue eyes measured him. "Are you aware of what your countryman says?"

"I saw him capture the man with the bloodstained knife, but I haven't spoken to him."

"He says that the man he attacked had previously plunged his knife into a colleague of his," the police officer said. "It is true that there was an attack on a sergeant in the United States forces. It is also true that the miscreant's knife is bloody."

"That would seem to settle it."

"No doubt this sergeant was justified," the police officer said, looking Ken up and down as if he were inspecting brand-new merchandise. "It is also true that the other sergeant had insulted the one who stabbed him."

"How do you know?"

"The prisoner has told me."

"That doesn't make it a fact."

The police officer's face grew red. "I have gone to great pains to assure you that I do not regard *your* countryman as a liar. Can you not do the same for me?"

Ken pursed his lips at this example of Asiatic logic, and hesitated before making an answer. "A man has been knifed," he said.

"True, but no disposition of the matter can recall those wounds." The officer sat back and put both hands across his paunch. The sight of an overweight man in a wartorn country was genuinely offensive to the eye, but Ken couldn't do anything about it.

He asked, "Are you letting the man with the knife go free?"

"He has already been freed."

Ken turned to the sergeant, explaining what had happened and being careful to add, "Don't let them see you get in an uproar about it."

But the Regular Army man bristled. "Why the hell not? Who do these gooks think they are, letting somebody who stabbed one of ours get away with it? And after everything we're doing for those goddamn—"

The police officer had started to get up threateningly from back of the desk, his Asiatic calm deserting him in the presence of foreigners.

Ken said to the sergeant, "Let's make tracks or we'll both get clobbered."

He heard a mighty cheer surge up from several dozen raw throats somewhere on the outside. The cheering continued as he and the sergeant began to leave, but it stopped abruptly when the two of them came out. Ken's eyes swiftly searched out Ha Binh, and he saw her with both hands up and her eyes on the men who had been part of the committee that had gone inside to the police station. Ken's heart sank.

The street crowd had dissolved for the most part, and the sergeant was gone by the time Ken walked over to Ha Binh.

"You were cheering for them, weren't you?"

"Yes."

"You wanted that man with the knife to go free even though he had hurt another man?"

152

"I didn't want to know that one of my countrymen is in the hands of a foreigner."

"I see."

He would never have guessed that he'd wake up to what was happening around him when he was standing with this girl on a littered street after a near-riot. But he knew the score now. She might have been very fond of him, might even have been in love with him, but she couldn't help thinking like a Vietnamese first. She belonged to one camp, so to speak, and he belonged to a different one. They could meet and touch and even have an affair, but nothing could ever work between them on a long-term basis.

"Come on, Ha Binh," he said sadly. "Let's go back to that restaurant and finish our meal. I haven't paid up for it yet and I'm sure you wouldn't want a foreigner ducking out on his obligation to a hardworking Vietnamese."

"We will go back if you wish," said Ha Binh.

Twelve

MATT COLBERT led his wife into the auditorium. The rear rows were mostly filled, so he moved down toward the front. There were a couple of seats in the eighteenth row center, so they took them. Evelyn walked slowly and stiffly but gave him a rigid smile when he glanced at her to find out if she liked his choice.

Evelyn kept from slumping down in her seat as the movie unreeled. It was a comedy, but she didn't laugh. As a rule she laughed like a maniac at even an indifferent comedy, and Matt was so surprised this time to see that she was quiet, that his eyebrows almost jumped up to his hairline.

She tried to ask herself for the hundredth time just how she was going to tell her man that she wanted a divorce. She didn't know how she'd explain that it wasn't on account of anything he had done, but what had been done to her as well as (be honest, now!) what she had wanted from any decent source. She hadn't wanted to be raped, heaven knew, but she had wanted an affair.

She didn't deserve Matt, and there was no way for her to keep from thinking so.

A man back of them suddenly started shouting, and some tall fellow dressed in black except for a yellow breast handkerchief came over to the shouter and talked quietly. The shouter's eyes grew wide with shock; then he closed his thick lips hard and folded his hands tautly. Breast-handkerchief led him away and stood against the north wall, glancing around to see if any other signs of trouble had shown themselves.

Evelyn had decided on the words she'd use tonight when she would talk to her man and tell him exactly what had happened and why she felt she had to ask him for a divorce.

When they left the theater a couple of hours later, Matt directed her attention toward a man who was leaning against a chipped wooden fence at the right of it. He was a square-headed Vietnamese whose attitude reminded Evelyn of one of those Nazi German officers in an old film on Stateside television.

"That's the fellow who got thrown out of there," Matt said quietly to her. "He started shouting that he was putting a curse on somebody."

Evelyn's attention was distracted from the major problem. "Moviegoing in Vietnam isn't like what I'm used to."

Matt grew rigid. "Don't look now, but he's walking in our direction. Let's move a little faster and ditch him."

He set his jaw and walked firmly, not missing a single step or going any faster than his normal walking speed. At the crest of a small hill, he glanced back. His eyes narrowed and blood seemed to be draining out of both lips. When he turned back, though, he made his voice level. "He's still back there."

"Do you think he's following us? It seems so ridiculous."

"In this country, nothing is. Well, let's ignore him."

"Don't you want to tell the police?"

Matt smiled frostily. "An SF lieutenant bitching to a Viet cop that another Viet is walking on the same block with him and his wife? If you can't imagine the response, I certainly can."

"What'll we do?"

He finally shrugged. "We aren't being hurt in any way, so let's roll with it."

"Is that the only thing we can do?"

"I'll figure something else, eventually," he said. "Until then, we've got three on a second honeymoon."

They dined quietly, and when they got out of the restaurant they saw the square-headed man leaning against a pole, his legs crossed. The Swiss-cheese-colored moon showed him wearing a gray topcoat, a gray pair of pants, and a hat to match.

They took a taxi to Evelyn's hotel, but when Matt looked out the window half an hour after getting there, the same man was in front of the place. Matt said he wasn't, of course, wanting to soothe her; but Evelyn looked out to make sure and saw him.

"What does he really want?" she whispered.

"Money. If he gets some he'll go away and stop trying to call down curses on our heads."

"Why does he pick on us?"

"All Americans are millionaires," Matt said soberly. "If I didn't happen to be on R and R, he might have picked you alone for his attentions."

Evelyn shuddered uncontrollably.

"I know you've missed me, dear," Matt said, for once misinterpreting her reaction.

"Matt, you don't understand! There's something I have to—"

"Can't it wait?"

She saw the wanting in his eyes, and she didn't mention it again. But she decided she'd definitely bring it up on the next day. It was only fair that he should know.

He made love to her that night, probably assuming that her remembered fright of that foul Vietnamese in the old house was actually her way of showing that she had been hungry for him all this time and that she wanted him. And when he was part of her, Evelyn realized that she did want him and had wanted him all the time. Matt was a good lover, kind, gentle, never domineering, but making his wishes known in such a way that she genuinely wanted to do what he liked.

The square-headed man was still in front of the hotel when they stepped out on the next morning. Matt took a different attitude this time and nodded at the fellow, smiling as he did it. The man couldn't have cared less. His face didn't change.

156

"Aren't you going to do something about him?" she asked.

"He's not hurting either of us," Matt remarked, "and if he's still at it before I have to leave, I'll think of something."

"I wish you'd give him money so he'd go away."

"If I did that, he'd come back later when you're alone."

The stranger might have made their week of rest not as comfortable as it might have otherwise been, but his presence nearby also kept Evelyn from telling Matt about the divorce she thought she wanted. She couldn't bring herself to add that much to his other worries. In the tension that the stranger caused she wanted to be loved by Matt.

And there was nothing easier for her than following Matt's directions. He simply ignored the man, and that seemed the end of it as far as he was concerned.

On the fifth day the square-headed man was still near them. And on the sixth. She thought she saw Matt's jaw jutting out with anger when he spotted the man on the sixth day, but Matt didn't say anything about what was on his mind, and Evelyn didn't ask any questions. She had enjoyed the leave enormously except for the square-headed man's presence close by, and she didn't want to remind him about what was wrong.

"I got out of bed last night and looked out the window," Matt told her while they were walking, "and there he was, on the job as usual. He must figure that when we get jumpy he'll be in for a whopping payoff."

On their sixth night together they made love with all the desperation of two people who knew that they might just possibly not ever see one another again and who wanted nothing more than to keep each other forever. In spite of their passion, neither Evelyn nor Matt enjoyed this night. They lay in each other's arms, apparently at peace with themselves, but it was close to four o'clock in the morning before Evelyn could drop off.

At half-past seven she went with him to the taxi that

would take him and his few belongings to the airport. He didn't plan for her to go to the airport with him and had made the point clear. She was so used to doing what he wanted that she agreed without putting up an argument.

As they walked into the fresh air again, she saw the square-headed man. He was leaning against a pole. He didn't seem to have changed his clothes since they had seen him for the first time.

Matt chuckled. "He must figure this is when he gets his payoff."

"You have to do something," she whispered.

"I'll take good care of him."

He turned and walked to his right, not stopping until he reached a point directly in front of the square-headed man. Evelyn could see only the strong betel-colored face with the mocking smile as he realized Matt was coming over to him. Then the face became rigid and hard and there was a second when she would have sworn that the eyes became childishly wide, and then the man suddenly turned and ran down the wide tree-shaded street. Matt was smiling softly when he came back to her.

"He won't bother you again," Matt said.

"What did you tell him?"

"I said that he had been very good to us to protect us during this last week, and that he was a typical example of Vietnamese friendliness and thoughtfulness."

"If that's the case, why did he run?"

"Because I told him I hoped he'd stay long enough to confirm an idea of mine. I said that I thought my wife wanted to leave me—she'd been a little distrait this last week—and that if he found out the truth for me he should let me know right away. I was going to give him a mail address, but he turned and ran. He realized he was actually welcome instead of being feared, so he said he would curse me forever and that was the end of it."

She asked cautiously, "You don't seriously think I would want to . . . ?"

"No, I don't." He added casually, "Should I think so?"

It was her chance to tell him, the opportunity she had been waiting for all week. But a cab was waiting and he was on his way to the Tan Son Nhut airport, on the way to a vicious and dirty war.

"No, dear, of course not," she said fervently. "Of course not."

They kissed briefly, both spent of passion after last night. She watched him get into the cab, not looking back of him. She waved at the cab until it was out of sight. Then she turned back to the hotel.

Next time, she would tell him. She'd never forget what had happened to her at the hands of one Vietnamese and that she was soiled all over. Next time she would tell him about it and let him decide whether he still wanted her.

Next time. There would have to be a next time, she decided.

The boy had tried to open a coconut, and a mine buried inside the coconut shell had gone off. It hadn't worked perfectly, but well enough to make the child with the damaged face another Vietcong victim.

Nina Field had worked on the boy for seven hours, grafting skin from other areas on his body. He was the fourth case she had taken on for the day, and she wanted to do her best, but the three others had all been luxury surgery for people who didn't really need it. As a result, when an important case came along, she was damnably tired and had to work much harder to do her best.

David Lawlor had phoned once, but she'd had no time to talk with him and had sent somebody else to do it. Lawlor left a message that he'd seen her before his leave was up. Nina hoped so. She wouldn't have married Dave Lawlor on a bet, but she certainly liked him.

Nina was kept busy by various cases, her own and others that had to be covered. Some were emergencies and important, but the ones that gave the most trouble involved middle-aged women with local influence who were in postoperative after having had their nostrils tilted

159

slightly or crowsfeet removed from under the eyes. Those cases were purely and simply hell on wheels. The war wounded always behaved so much better.

She didn't hear from Lawlor during the next day or the day after. A call put through to the nearest U.S. forces billet brought her the information that Sergeant Lawlor was registered but his room wasn't in use.

He must have found himself some other girl, Nina decided. Next time she saw him she'd give him hell in a quiet way.

When Lawlor phoned on the following morning Nina said that she couldn't see him at all. She kept cool about it, not hinting that she was upset in any way. She said that she was going to be on duty during the night.

Lawlor snapped, "So long, baby," and hung up.

Nina waited a full minute before she let go of the telephone. She had found that work was a certain cure for any emotional hang-up, so she asked to take over the emergency section for that night. Dr. Kabatchnik, his gray jowls sagging wearily, agreed and then thanked her for volunteering.

At half-past four in the morning, Dave Lawlor was hauled into the emergency section. Two men had to bring him in. His face was one big bandage except for the eyes and nostrils. His hands were the color of fire. Nina recognized that big, bearlike build as soon as she saw it. No army was likely to have more than one man like Dave Lawlor.

"I took me on a couple of Charlies," Lawlor said when he had eased himself into a chair. "There was a chick with them, and she turned out pretty rough, too. She came across once I got both hands around her throat, but I didn't really get a boot out of it. Not like when I'm with you, baby."

"Sit back and don't brag so much. Now roll up your right sleeve. This won't hurt any more than you deserve."

"What the hell are you doing?"

"I'm putting you to sleep first of all, as there's nothing

seriously wrong with you. In the morning, we'll see what minor things have to be attended to."

"You mean I might have to spend the rest of my leave in this dump?" But he was grinning. "With you to take care of me? By God, army life sure is hell, ain't it?"

"Don't count chickens," Nina said primly. "Before they're hatched, I mean. *You* know."

"Sure I know, baby." Lawlor was still grinning. "I hope that a fellow in my delicate condition can snag himself a private room."

"You won't be in condition for anything until tomorrow."

"We'll need a private room tomorrow, so you might as well get me one for tonight, too."

Nina sighed. "I suppose so, you arrogant bastard."

PART FOUR

Thirteen

THE BASE had been under attack in a small way for the last two and a half nights, Matt Colbert was able to tell his team in an hour after they had got back. The VC, with or without the help of North Viet troops, were getting ready to make it hot for Tam Hung.

Dave Lawlor asked confidently, "How do we stop 'em?"

"Let's wait till nighttime before deciding, so we can see just how bad the situation is," Matt Colbert said. "Meanwhile we've got work to do."

Dave asked, "We're not just going to let Charlie get away with shooting our asses off, are we, sir?"

"When I decide on letting Charlie get away with anything, Sergeant," Matt said crisply, "you'll be the first one I tell about it. Now will you Goddamn well get to work!"

It was Sid Wheeler who first found out that something wasn't right in the village. It happened because he made a point of moving from hut to hut after his daily medical lineup and asking if there happened to be any extra health problems. At the hut of Co See, the married woman with whom Ken Hubbard's Viet chick had been living, Wheeler found one of the kids sick in bed. He ministered to the kid as best he was able, shooting her full of aspirin and leaving some goo, along with instructions. Before he was finished, Co See had come back to the hut. She was in a stew, rubbing her hands together and looking at Wheeler as if the colored medic were getting ready to chop her head off.

Wheeler said accusingly, "The child has been ill for several days. Why wasn't the medical officer notified?"

"I have not been able to pay for medicines."

"Don't you know that these things are free?"

"But I thought . . ." Co See began. "I mean—I thought that the new rules meant . . ."

Wheeler, who'd been shutting his med bag, looked sharply across the room at her. "What new rules?"

"The Dai Dien has announced that as of last week, the government will have to take a fee for all medical treatments."

Wheeler kept from spitting with anger. "We'll forget about the fee this time, and if anything happens you'll let me know and we'll arrange something between ourselves."

He left and sought out Chris Ablett. There had been a short spell of rain, and he found Ablett sitting under a couple of ponchos lashed together and raised with sticks. The lieutenant was trying to shape his boots with the help of black medical tape and telephone wire; any item made of leather wasn't likely to hold up very long in Vietnam weather.

"What's the story, Sergeant?" Ablett demanded.

"The Dai Dien is charging money for medical treatments," Wheeler burst out. "Every day since we left, I suppose, he's been collecting from people we've helped for free."

Ablett brushed his cheeks with the tips of his fingers. "We'd better let Matt—uh, the captain know about this. I don't like it a damn bit."

Matt Colbert, who was back at the base CP and in conversation with his Vietnamese counterpart, Dac Hee Quang, looked annoyed at the interruption. But he heard the men out and then turned to his counterpart.

"Would you know anything about this?" he asked in Vietnamese.

"No." Dac Hee Quang looked worried. "We cannot question his authority. The Dai Dien is the man sent over by the government."

163

"He's a Goddamn thief," Matt said roughly. "Then I take it you won't raise hell with the bastard?"

"My hands are tied."

"Mine aren't." Matt raised them till they were parallel with his head, as if to prove the point literally. He glanced over at Ablett. "Where's Lawlor?"

"On a demo job, Captain."

"I'll want him with me on this caper," Matt decided. "There's nothing like the presence of a big ox like Lawlor to help persuade somebody into doing what you want."

Matt and Lawlor found the Dai Dien standing spread-legged in the middle of the biggest room in the concrete building where he lived and worked. The Dai Dien was shifting a cigar around in his mouth. The clothes he wore had been well made and recently cleaned and ironed. There probably wasn't a spot of dirt in the room.

"Yes, Captain?" he asked Matt silkily as soon as he saw the newcomers. "You catch me at a busy time, but I will leave all else aside in order to talk with you."

Matt said bluntly, "You've been stealing your people blind."

"I? Captain, I work most hard in this village. I am planning to put up a shrine, which the people feel that they need. And many other—"

"To put it up with whose money?"

"I wouldn't have felt that it matters," the Dai Dien said blandly, "but if you must know the people are collecting among themselves. I felt that in order to give them some pride and make them feel that the shrine is really their own, then it is necessary—"

"And of course, the money is in your charge and you'll clip off a few million p-notes for yourself."

"The money is in charge of Tran Dong Hoa, who is a man of great age and caution." The Dai Dien blinked twice. "Do you think that I would steal money for a shrine?"

"You'd steal the pennies from a dead man's eyes," Matt said bluntly. "You're charging the people for medical

164

treatments which are free, and you know damn well they're being paid for by my government."

"A slight misunderstanding." The Dai Dien shrugged. "The people misunderstood an announcement of mine, I feel sure. Not many of the villagers are able to read, as you certainly know."

Matt knew it because he and Ablett had been trying to teach reading. It was a job that not even Matt, who felt sure he could do anything he put his mind to, enjoyed very much. As for Chris Ablett, he was a patient man, but that particular job took too much out of him and he hated it.

"Very well, then," Matt said. "I take it that the money will be refunded to the various villagers."

"That I cannot do, Captain. As soon as the money was received, I fear, it was spent. There are numerous expenses at Tam Hung and—"

"Then I expect you to make full restitution in, let's say, one week."

"Captain, as one educated man to another I throw myself on your mercy." The Dai Dien swallowed. "I have many debts to pay at Danang and Dalat, many expenses."

"Women?"

"And gambling," the Dai Dien admitted, hanging his head. When he looked up he was smiling. "After all, Captain, how much harm have I done? The money has only been taken away from ignorant persons with no capacity to use it intelligently, and I may even have done them a favor by relieving them of necessary decisions."

Matt rubbed his hands fiercely and then said, "Well, I'm willing to forget the whole thing provided it never happens again and provided you make full restitution and behave yourself from now on."

"But Captain, I have just explai——"

"Yes, but the workings of chance may be as mysterious to you as they are to us all, and perhaps I can clarify them. For example, Sergeant Lawlor is prone to drink a good deal."

165

Lawlor didn't show that he was surprised, his intake of liquor being only moderate so he could keep himself in good shape. But he took it for granted the captain was carrying a few cards up his sleeve, and so he let it pass.

"In the course of a drinking bout, Sergeant Lawlor might wander too close to your home, and if you should be on the premises he might just possibly become belligerent. Do you follow me?"

"Is this a threat?" the Dai Dien asked, drawing himself up to his full five feet eight.

"Only between educated men," Matt Colbert said smoothly.

The Dai Dien looked at Lawlor and then turned away. "Unless I mend my ways to agree with yours," he said, "I face the threat of this—this . . ."

"Sergeant Lawlor is an honest man who dislikes to see cheating at any level."

The Dai Dien closed his eyes briefly, probably imagining his own feelings after a few minutes with Dave Lawlor. "Very well," he said. "The money shall be returned."

"Within a week, please."

"But I told you that I have debts."

"We all do," Matt Colbert said. "The world is difficult for those of us who like to spend money."

"Very well, Captain," the Dai Dien said frigidly. "The money shall be returned on this day. You have my word on it. May I now ask a favor?"

"Of course."

"Good. I have no wish to see or speak to you for as long as you remain in Tam Hung. That will be all."

Matt's lips were pursed when he got out of there. The Dai Dien would probably send a stinger about Matt over to the people above him, and Matt knew he'd have to take time out to send a report of his own just as quickly as he could.

Being unable to talk with the Dai Dien worked to his disadvantage during the day. When something came up, he had to send Chris Ablett over to see the man. He knew that for him to send one of the sergeants would be considered such a great insult that he'd be swiftly taken out of this village after what he might do became known to his people or the Dai Dien's higher-ups.

Toward evening Ken Hubbard came to him with a new worry. Matt had been counting the number of five-gallon resupply cans of water dosed with iodine, but he stopped himself as soon as he got one look at Hubbard's face. It was drawn and he seemed even thinner than before.

"Sergeant, how was the leave?" Matt asked, hoping to put him at ease.

"All right, sir. And yours?"

"Nearly perfect. Did you bring the girl back with you? The one you took out there?"

"No, I talked her into staying in Saigon, for a while at least."

Ken winced, remembering his last sight of Ha Binh, tears in her eyes but standing upright with straight back and even the start of a smile on her thin face.

"What's wrong, Sergeant?" Matt asked. "You look like you had your nuts shot off."

"It's almost like that, sir, in a way. I hate to see the villagers get a beating. You know that we've promised to build a new shrine for the people as soon as they get the material together for it."

"What about about the shrine?" Matt looked startled.

"The villagers have been raising money among themselves and keeping it in the hands of an elder named Tran Hong Hoa. Tonight he was coming back to his hut with food supplies, when he saw a man running away from his hut. Tran is old and can't see too well, but he swears the man wasn't dressed in black pajamas, like every other man is around here, and wasn't wearing a military uniform either."

"I suppose the money was gone."

Ken nodded slowly.

"The Dai Dien has been busy, hasn't he?" Matt said morosely. "And if I go over there and try to get the money

167

back, he'll tell me I can't find it, and he'll have hidden it so his own mother couldn't get hold of it without his okay."

"I suppose you're right, sir."

"What's even worse, the hell-raising about something I can't prove will make me subject to dismissal from Tam Hung, and the South Viet government is pretty sure to blackball me anyplace else in the country where I might be sent."

"Have you got any plans, sir?"

"Sergeant, I'm a little surprised you can't guess," Matt said, cheering up. "First of all, I'm going to see the Dai Dien. You can come with me. This isn't going to be a muscle job."

They took a jeep into the village, driving carefully, as everybody had to do between cities. Ken was at the wheel, his eyes apparently in front and behind the car as well as at the sides, and all seemingly at the same time. Matt always watched Ken Hubbard at the wheel as if he couldn't believe what he was seeing. He guessed that Ken Hubbard's patience was what made the Kentuckian such a good demolition man, but it certainly took more in the way of patience than Matt was ever likely to have.

The Dai Dien was probably in bed; as much as ten minutes passed before the door opened on one eye and a triangular wedge of skin leading down to thin lips. As soon as he saw who was outside the Dai Dien tried to shut the door, but Matt had already eased a foot between the frame and threshold. The Dai Dien stepped back, allowing Matt to come in. At his gestures, Ken Hubbard followed and shut the door. He locked it of his own free will, but Matt didn't complain.

"I asked not to see you again or to have to speak to you," the Dai Dien started. "For this breach of manners, I will write out a complaint and send it to my superiors."

"Don't crap a crap artist, pal," Matt said easily. "You needed money and you took what you needed, so we've got us a standoff."

168

"Pardon?" But the Dai Dien's eyes were narrowing and he was thinking quickly.

"If you get rid of me I pass the whole story about the shrine money to your superiors and mine, and to the villagers." He smiled. "How long can you stay here with no one on your side? Damned if I know, but it can't be too long."

"There is no proof—"

"There's one man's testimony."

"A nearly blind old man."

"It'll be easy to get proof that your gambling debts have been suddenly paid off, and I don't think your government is going to ignore this little riff of yours, pal, or slap your wrist for it, either. And if you thought so you'd have kicked me out of here by now. Right? Right. So here's the story, pal—I have to let you get away with the shrine money, and you have to keep shut about me. That way nobody complains and we're back to doing business as usual."

The Dai Dien nodded slowly. "Then I am to speak to you whether I want to or not. Is that so?"

"We're stuck with each other," Matt Colbert said soberly. "Besides, we work better if we can be in direct touch and without obstructions."

The Dai Dien nodded again. He'd have been grateful for a chance to do anything physical, the more strenuous the better; but all he could do in the face of repeated insults and un-Asian bluntness was to keep nodding.

Matt said gravely, "Thank you for having consented to see me."

The Dai Dien was quiet. Matt turned around and left, waiting just outside till Ken Hubbard joined him.

"Let's scoot back to base," he said. "It's nighttime, and something's bound to be popping if I know Charlie."

Fourteen

MARY TREEN was sobbing. The tears rolled off her smooth young cheeks and down to the gray uniform of a probationary nurse. She rocked back and forth in the hard chair next to Nina Field's desk on the third floor of the U.S. Hospital in Saigon.

"That—that sweet boy," Mary gasped through her tears. "He was so nice-looking, so sweet when he was brought in, so kind, so young and handsome."

She sobbed a little more loudly, remembering how many times she had imagined herself helping that young soldier by bringing him medicine, saving him from a relapse, nursing him to final recovery, and—and then marrying him. Mary Treen couldn't help it if she still had some romantic ideas. She was only twenty-three years old.

"And then at two o'clock I saw Doctor Passy leaving the room and the men from downstairs come to take him. A sweet boy like that!"

"We lost Corporal Hirsch half an hour ago, yes." Nina nodded. "Don't you believe that everybody did the best for him?"

"I suppose so, but I couldn't s-stand it if I ever got so mixed up and it happened again. I'm getting out of this job and maybe out of nursing altogether."

Nina sighed, having seen more than her share of this sort of thing. Young girls thought it was feminine to be sensitive, so they sometimes carried on as if a single reverse had finished everything for them. Sometimes a girl actually developed a powerful repulsion against the work, and one single case could change her whole life. Nina doubted whether Mary Treen was putting on an act,

170

though, and hoped that her own successor would get hold of a replacement quickly.

Nina had decided to quit her own job, too. Not for the same reason, of course, but because she'd had too much of currying favor, of doing things that weren't necessary in order to have a chance at saving lives.

"Well, think it over," she said pleasantly, "and let me or Matron know what you decide."

Mary Treen was still sobbing when she left the office.

There was a Viet girl who was supposed to see Nina, probably one of the million goof-offs who wanted a useless operation. At the very idea, Nina grew rigid with fury and a cord pulsed at the right side of her neck.

The girl who walked in was trying not to seem scared. Her little chin was thrust out determinedly. She smiled but couldn't keep her lips from twitching at the corners. Her hands were raised to a point just below her shoulders, as if she was hoping to ward off a blow. Her face was pretty, even though there wasn't a suspicion of makeup on it.

Behind her came Mrs. Jenner, a dried-up-looking woman who would interpret for both of them. Mrs. Jenner and her husband had lived in this country from the days when the French ran it, and some jokers at the hospital claimed that she and her husband talked Vietnamese when they were in bed.

Mrs. Jenner said dryly, "This girl came out to Saigon because she claimed she needed hospital care, but in the last few days she's become a lot better."

"Can I see a file card on her, please?"

The girl was called Ha Binh, Nina noted. She and the girl looked at each other, and each talked in a language that the other didn't understand. Neither one spared a glance at Mrs. Jenner during the conversation, but waited patiently for the older woman's translation.

"You are well, Ha Binh, but you claim that you require hospital care."

"I do not require care."

"Now that you are talking with a doctor, you admit the truth."

171

"Someone else claimed that I needed hospital care, not me."

"You realize, of course, that you will be sent back to the village from which you came."

The girl surprised Nina by saying, "I want to go back, yes. I have decided to go back."

"Why? There is more danger on the outskirts than in this city or Danang or Dalat."

The girl's cheeks reddened and her eyes were lowered. "You think that I want to escape, to have nothing to do with what is happening to my people. I've lost a husband, but I have to . . ."

"You have to go back?"

"Yes. And I need a medical clearance from you in order to do so. That is why I came here today."

"Then you want me to send you to what may be your death?" Nina's face was white. "You don't have any right to ask me for that."

"Do you have the right to refuse?"

Nina sat back. Her eyes and the girl's were locked in what seemed like mortal combat.

Ha Binh said more quietly, "I don't know what I can do, but I want the chance to try. Such a thing is most important to me. I can't let my country die and feel that I've done nothing at all to help."

"Very well," Nina said heavily. She turned to Mrs. Jenner. "Give her what she wants and sign my name to any forms that need to be filled out. Say that she has undergone a course of treatment at the hospital and been cured of illness. Don't let me see her again. I—I want to think for a while."

Ha Binh seemed to have understood the drift of Nina's decision long before Mrs. Jenner started to translate for her benefit. She nodded gently in Nina's direction and said, "Thank you very much."

Nina closed her eyes. "First you ask me to help you kill yourself, and then you thank me for it."

Ha Binh said softly, "To fight for what you believe in is a privilege."

172

When Nina opened her eyes again, as much as five minutes later, both Ha Binh and Mrs. Jenner had left the office. She folded her hands and let herself give some thought to what had just happened. The talk with that girl had helped Nina Field change her mind about her own job.

She had come out to this country to help, but it had proved not easy to help. The people themselves made it hard for her in dozens of ways big and little. But if the helping was worthwhile she had to stick it out. If one case in fifty was worth handling, if she saved one life and preserved one future, then what she did was worth all the drawbacks. Without her, there was some chance that one important case in fifty might get fluffed off.

Nina stood up, the decision made. She would stay in Saigon and see this through for as long as she could. And she'd try her damnedest not to complain uselessly about the bad things that were sure to go on all around her. She would try and save her strength for the times when it would be needed.

She left the room and hurried out to find Mary Treen, determined to talk the young probationary nurse into staying at the hospital as well. There couldn't be too many people out here trying to do the best that was in them.

Fifteen

MATT COLBERT stood spread-legged some fifteen feet from the outer perimeter of barbed wire at the base. There was a gaping hole in front of him. At the right of it was a human foot with part of a pants leg and a shoe. The soldier had been blown out of sight.

"A Bouncing Betty mine," Matt said soberly. "Some Charlie must have sneaked in here and buried the Goddamn thing, and when this guy stepped on it he lost out."

Matt peered past the barbed wire. Every so often a lighted flare would show him a network of grubby trees that hid malarial mosquitoes, snakes, flies, and even warrior ants who tried to eat their way to the base of the human brain.

Back of him was a rectangle of sandbags and mud walls. A sheath of barbed wire and claymore mines barricaded a pair of 4.2 mortar pits and four machine-gun bunkers, one at each corner. Tunnels had been dug in back of them, including a dispensary that could be used in emergencies and a communications room. The ceiling logs would squeak whenever somebody walked above them, but the chances of a cave-in were rated as pretty small, and it was a good place to catch a few winks between tours of outpost duty.

Matt looked grim. This planted mine was different from the usual sniper fire at night and the occasional mortar barrage that would be answered swiftly.

Dave Lawlor, who stood nearby with Ken Hubbard, said, "Charlie is damn well asking for it this time."

Matt nodded. "I'm taking a patrol out there for a look

174

around. Sergeant Lawlor, we'll need some sixty men for this one."

"Yes, sir. CIDGs, but better than nothing."

Matt nearly smiled. Lawlor didn't think of the Civil Irregular Defense Groups as professional fighters, even though he admitted that they were pretty good. The Jeh tribesmen had only recently put away loincloths and crossbows and taken up tiger suits and M-16 rifles. Besides, their families lived in cave bunkers, their bare-breasted women worked the fields, and most of them saw their children nearly every day and could quit the service whenever they wanted to. Lawlor had never heard of such arrangements before, so he didn't trust them to turn out first-class fighting men.

"Much better than nothing," Matt said. "And I'll want you on the job with me."

"Yes, Captain." Lawlor smiled. "Always a pleasure to work with you, sir."

The patrol was no different from many others, Matt decided as he walked fifteen feet from the nearest man. They groped their way through thickets or muddy water almost up to the eyes, every man knowing he'd be shot at. Then there would be a few shots. The men would answer. It would become quiet again. The patrol would keep going.

The only sounds that anybody could hear for a while were those of the men slogging ahead and the noises of crickets and other night sounds in a hostile land. Every man knew that if the kraits didn't kill, for instance, the traps might. If the traps didn't, Charlie or his pals in the NVA were a good bet to try and do the job.

Just before they reached a stop point, one soldier got his leg caught in a punji trap. Matt, who was nearest, had to overrule his first impulse of getting the man out. Instead he probed the trap gently, searching for a grenade that might well be under it to make for a double trap. He found nothing. By the time he removed the man's foot from the trap, the Viet medic told him that an infection

175

had set in. The man's buddies had to stretch a poncho across bamboo sticks and carry him.

Matt spoke to Lawlor for a while during the pause. Lawlor had found a natural cover and was heating his C-rations with a special tablet. The blue flame gave his hard face a devilish look.

"What the hell do you suppose Charlie is waiting for?" Lawlor asked, completely out of sorts.

"He'll show up," Matt said dryly.

"I hope you're right, sir. I hate this tear-assing around after him all the time. If he'd just stand the hell in one place and fight, we could—"

"Charlie doesn't work like that, Lawlor. I'd advise you to fight the war that's going on instead of the one that you'd prefer."

"Yes, Captain," Lawlor said automatically. But he didn't look convinced.

The patrol started up again. Nothing happened for twenty minutes, and Matt wondered if Charlie or his NVA pals hadn't lost track of them. If that was the case, the patrol was likely to be a hundred percent useless.

Ahead of him, the point man suddenly staggered, having fallen across a bamboo pole. A mine sent earth into the air behind him and popped a number of grenades strung from branches.

Matt's counterpart, Dac Hee Quang, who was in command of the operation, shouted, "Drop!"

Machine-gun fire opened up against them and out of sight. Quang calmly directed fire ahead of the patrol and on both flanks. Men called out for medical help.

"Ammunition," somebody shouted. "Bring it here."

Somebody else shouted, "Where's my foot? My foot!"

A fifteen-yard-wide perimeter had been set up in spite of darkness. Single shots were coming at the men from two sides. Matt saw some men digging frenziedly while others covered them.

Quang, under heavy fire, was giving orders to his radioman. Lawlor, hurling hand grenades as if they were baseballs, took time to watch the Viet radioman's work and nod back at Matt. There would be air power on the way soon enough.

By Matt's guess it took twelve minutes before a pair of Phantom jets roared in just above the treetops, dropping napalm on the first pass and fragmentation bombs on the second.

Over the hellish roar, Matt managed to make himself heard by Quang. "Closer," he shouted. "Get it in closer."

Quang nodded, then gave instructions to his radioman. The man hesitated, shuddering, and then put through the orders he had been given. The next air strike came in a number of yards closer. The earth shivered. There was nothing to do for a while except keep on living, and Matt knew he was lucky he could do that.

The last attack had quieted Charlie down. Quang cleared his throat loudly and said, "Forward, all of you!"

Carefully the men moved out of the perimeter. That was when machine-gun fire started up once again. The enemy had been sticking close to the patrol, knowing it was their best hope to survive air strikes.

Matt heard the radioman shouting to the base through his machinery for a hoist lift to get critically wounded out of the area. The number of wounded must have been high. Even above the screams of machine-gun bullets and mortar shells and the whine and thunder of grenades, Matt could hear the shouts for medical aid.

And then every noise suddenly stopped for him. He had been in battle any number of times, of course, but had never gone deaf before. He was starting to wonder if he'd ever get normal hearing back again.

A soldier with a wound lay in a patch of clearing some eight feet away, his presence shown by a flare. Matt crawled over to him. The soldier gestured toward Matt's water canteen. Matt had it half-open before he realized that the soldier's wound was in the stomach. He doused two fingers with the stuff and traced the outline of the man's lips with the fingers, as if putting on makeup. He supposed he said something to the man, but he couldn't hear himself.

177

There was a line of wounded not far from him and one grim-faced soldier watching over them. His canteen had been overturned, empty because it had been used by so many of the men. Matt passed his own canteen over.

He was making his way to Quang, when he saw a gray flick in the darkness near him and knew a grenade had landed. He didn't hesitate, but reached down to grab it and throw it into the distance. There was a moment of fiery light and somebody in an NVA uniform had his mouth open and rigid.

One of the soldiers gestured toward Matt's first-aid kit. Matt took it off but saw that the soldier at the other one's feet was dead. He pulled the kit back and handed it to somebody else in need. The soldier who'd asked for it first grew angry and started to lunge at Matt, but an oncoming mortar shell made all of them duck for cover. When the angry soldier looked back he saw that his dead friend's body had been blasted to pieces.

By flare light, Matt could see Quang studying a map and probably giving orders to his radioman, directing the strikes to come. Air strikes had been almost continuous, but it seemed that more of them were going to be necessary.

He was ten feet from Quang, but when he ducked for a grenade burst, the damn thing practically picked him up and hurled him in Quang's direction. As soon as the dust had cleared he had to run only five or six feet toward his Viet counterpart. He found Quang sitting straddle-legged on the ground, squinting into the darkness.

Matt gestured that he couldn't hear. The Viet Captain nodded, then pointed past the perimeter. There was a light made by gun bullets and Matt realized that a machine-gun nest wasn't far from them.

"I think I can fix that if I've got help." Matt threw his head back. "Sergeant! Lawlor!"

It didn't surprise him that the sergeant heard himself being called. He was at Matt's elbow in a minute, face flushed, eyes dancing.

178

Matt shouted, "Machine-gun nest over there. What say we finish it off?"

Lawlor grinned and clapped his hands exultantly. Not until Matt heard the sergeant's hands clap did he realize that his hearing was better now. He guessed that the recent contact with earth had joggled his skull so much that the hearing block had been cleared up. Actually he didn't give a damn how it had happened as long as he could hear again.

Matt and Lawlor started out, M-16s at the ready. The sergeant's grin hadn't left his face, Matt noticed, and he wondered idly what made a man like that enjoy the work he was doing. Lawlor would probably see a number of peace-loving men die horribly and envy them without exactly knowing why, but the fates would keep him alive and let him grow old and useless. He'd probably die in bed or at a Veterans Administration Hospital when he was in his seventies or eighties and feeling he had lived fifty years too long.

Matt's eyes raked the black strip of savage land as he moved, crouched and alert now that they were advancing farther into enemy territory. For some idiotic reason he was conscious of not having shaved and that his clothes had become rumpled and caked with dirt. His face was greasy with sweat that hadn't been wiped off. The backs of his eyes seemed to have dropped further down into his head.

A flare again, coming at exactly the wrong time. Matt and Lawlor stopped, exposed and cursing the Viets for not knowing when to lay off on the Goddamn flares.

It made no difference, though. They weren't noticed. A number of NVA men past the clearing were busily dragging bodies away and out of sight, vines tied to the dead ankles to identify the bodies as belonging to their side.

Matt and Lawlor had been flanking the machine-gun nest, and as they moved another row of bullets stitched the darkness at their side.

Matt hurled a grenade pointblank at the gun nest. There was a weak noise of thudding, as if he had thrown a rock.

"Goddamn dud," he muttered under his breath.

The gun-nest personnel were alive to their danger now. Bullets roared up and down the ground immediately in front of Lawlor and Matt, forcing them to scramble for cover behind the nearest trees.

Lawlor was all right, Matt saw out of the corner of an eye. He'd heard a pair of gasps, though, and Matt took it for granted that a couple of enemy had been close by and had caught it from their own men.

It was Lawlor who acted next, pulling the spoon out of a grenade and letting go. It was hard to tell, but Matt thought that the sergeant had hit the spot on the head. They waited, but no more gunfire came their direction.

Matt held up his left hand with thumb and second finger making a circle for victory. Lawlor waved back to show that he'd got the message.

When they started on the way to the perimeter they realized that the last grenade as well as the previous machine-gun fire must have alerted some enemy to their presence.

A rifle shot was fired from too close to them. Lawlor snarled, took a step backward, raised his rifle, and fired chest-high in the direction of the other bullet. He was cursing at the top of his lungs.

A volley of return shots followed. Lawlor called out with distress and fell. Two NVA men moved softly in darkness toward the fallen man, having started out just after Matt ducked around back of a tree.

Having drawn them out, Lawlor suddenly raised one hand to hurl a grenade. It was almost as if a hammer had landed on the two men, pushing them down to the ground. Dark as it was, they had been outlined against the sky, but at the grenade's impact they simply disappeared.

"You've got the guts of a burglar, pal," Matt said. "I only hope you don't go too far one of these days."

It surprised him that Lawlor should have heard it.

"Not a chance, Captain," Lawlor said, keeping his voice low. "I'm in-de-Goddamn-structible, that's what I am."

At that moment an NVA man jumped out from behind a tree and plunged straight at Matt, who crushed the rifle stock down across the man's head. The man didn't call out or gasp or give any sign that he'd been touched; but he suddenly stopped moving. Matt drew back, and the NVA man fell directly forward, as straight and stiff and hard as a sawed-under tree. He fell at a point halfway between Matt and Lawlor.

"You going to let him live, sir?" Lawlor asked quietly.

"No." Matt reached for the M-16, which had dropped out of his hand. He fired once. The NVA man's head turned into a bloody pulp.

As soon as Matt took a step forward he realized that his left arm had gone dead on him. He couldn't help letting an oath escape him.

The sergeant asked, "You all right, sir?"

"That son of a bitch had a knife and knew how to use it," Matt said. "The left arm got it. But I'll be okay if we get out of this."

"*When* we get out," Lawlor said savagely, then added, "sir."

Matt snapped, "Haul your ass out of here and don't waste time choosing words."

But he let Lawlor take the lead and covered as best he could. The sergeant moved swiftly as a snake. It struck Matt as eerie that in spite of gunfire and even mortar shells it was possible to hear animal noises and especially those damn crickets.

The wound in Matt's arm was making it hard for him to think straight, and he didn't know at exactly what moment he was at the perimeter and back of it. Only vaguely did he remember having to sit still while a medic anxiously applied some gook to his wound before dressing it in an elaborate bandage. The medic, a birdlike little man, told Matt it wouldn't be long before he was on his way to a hospital.

181

"Piss on that," Matt growled. "Where's Quang?"

"But you shouldn't—" the medic started.

"I'll find him myself."

He picked his way carefully among the wounded and the hurrying and the confused and the frightened. Quang had been talking to Dave Lawlor, but as soon as Matt appeared he rushed over to shake Matt's good hand.

"What's the situation now?" Matt asked, passing over Quang's first remarks.

Quang swallowed. "They are trying to get through our line. Many of them have stolen uniforms from soldiers of ours and some have certainly got through."

"What are we doing about it?"

"Killing those who seem suspicious," Quang said blandly. "I suppose that we've killed some of our own, but there's no help for it in the circumstances."

Matt and Lawlor looked at each other, but neither man said a word in criticism.

"Our scouts tell us that the enemy has a gun on wheels," Quang said. "A nine-man team is to go out and destroy it."

"Nine?"

"We can't spare much more than nine."

Matt nodded. "I wouldn't mind a piece of that action."

"Not in your condition, Captain." Quang smiled. "My regrets."

Matt nodded slowly. "All the same, if we land that particular swatch of equipment, Charlie might get good and clobbered before he can do a fade."

"That is most impossible."

"I've been out there already, so I know at least the feel of the territory. I think I could pretty well—"

"No, sir," Lawlor said. "I swear if you even try it I'll knock you clear to Tam Hung."

"Lawlor, I'll have your ass for this!"

"Sir, it's too much of a chance and you know it." He turned to Quang. "I'll be glad to go."

Quang said, "You know the dangers?"

"I do, yes. I've just been there."

"Your presence on this mission will be most welcome."

Lawlor rubbed his meaty, callused palms against each other. Matt, watching him briefly, grunted.

"Good luck, Sergeant," he said finally. "Think of me lazing around here while you're out there."

Lawlor grinned and faded from sight. Matt turned to Quang. "Have we got howitzers?"

"We do."

Matt nodded. The 105-millimeter jobs had been slingloaded under twin-turbined Chinook choppers and parachuted down. That would make some difference.

"I'll go over and see what I can do," Matt said. "You seem to have everything else pretty much in hand."

Quang nodded. "It depends, I think, on the mounted cannon."

"Maybe so."

Matt turned and hurried toward the perimeter. He was feeling better now that he was behind his lines. The arm stung every so often when he gave it too much of a move, but the pain wasn't so bad that he couldn't live with it.

He found the howitzer crew further from the perimeter than he would have preferred, but as he started to say something, one man caught a sniper's bullet. Matt dropped the sniper with a rifle shot and the aid of a flare, then hurried to help the others, using the bad arm as much as he could.

A signal to fire was given. Matt heard a *click!* and nothing more except the beginning of a blast. He never heard anything again.

Lawlor and the eight other men came back from their dangerous mission within an hour. Lawlor reported that the cannon on wheels had been wiped the hell out.

The enemy attack had already leveled off, and silence from the guns made nature sounds seem deafening.

Quang hesitated. "I have just received news of your captain."

Lawlor, about to pull back and get a few minutes of

rest, stopped himself and whirled around. "How bad?"

"Dead."

Lawlor shut his eyes for as long as twenty seconds. Then he opened them again, and in a voice that was a shade higher than he'd have liked it to be, he asked, "How did Charlie manage it?"

"The enemy didn't," Quang said. "One of the howitzer shells dropped short and killed an entire crew, including Captain Colbert."

Dave Lawlor said bitterly, "Charlie couldn't knock off Matt Colbert, so his own side had to do it."

That was probably the most bitter remark Dave Lawlor would ever make in his life.

Sixteen

THE LETTERS for Evelyn Colbert arrived three days after
the notification. Every one said that her husband had
been a good leader and an inspiration to his men and
he'd be missed. The letters had been written carefully
and the words obviously chosen after considerable thought.

Evelyn realized that the men were genuinely upset at
having lost their captain, but she didn't care how they
felt. She took every letter and tore it across and then
tore it into fourths and dropped it into the nearest waste-
basket. The letters had been written by men who were
alive, and they didn't have any right to be alive when
Matt was dead. To hell with every one of them!

She made arrangements to leave Vietnam and go back
to the States, choosing San Francisco because it was a
new city to her. If she liked it there, she'd be able to
start out all over again.

Once there, she found an inexpensive furnished apartment just off Geary Street. For the first few days she
went sightseeing, trying to get the feel of the city. She
rode the cable cars, spent an hour at Fisherman's Wharf,
took in a Chinese play with its noisy audience and spine-
tingling music. One afternoon she rented a car and drove
through the exclusive Russian Hill section.

She first had a near-fainting spell when she was on her
way back from that trip. Something she had been reading
in the *Chronicle* made her guess that the altitude was too
much for her. She went to a doctor, who took some tests.
A few days later he told her he had good news for her.
At least he hoped it was going to be considered good
news.

"Your illness, so-called, had nothing to do with the altitude," he said. "You're going to have a baby, Mrs. Colbert. The tests prove it. Congratulations."

At first she was overjoyed. There'd be a living remembrance of her Matt, a boy who'd grow up straight and strong. She'd work hard and try to raise him so that Matt would be proud if he could know what she was doing.

But lying in bed that night, she realized that it was possible for the child not to be Matt's. The father could very well be that foul and disgusting Vietnamese.

She had gone out to Vietnam to see her husband, had decided while waiting for him that she'd have an affair, and instead had been savagely raped. Maybe she had to pay a price for having wanted to be disloyal to Matt, and maybe the price would consist of the agony of worry before Matt's baby was born.

She didn't know the answer and realized that only after eight months was she going to find out. She didn't sleep for many nights of agonizing worry.

Seventeen

THE REPLACEMENT for Matt Colbert was due to arrive at
base before day's end. Chris Ablett, who would be in
charge till that time, was having some trouble with another replacement.

Not that there was anything wrong with Hugo Pearl's
work. He was a communications man cross-trained in
heavy weapons and demo work, the way Tom Dearden
had been. He was a hard and willing worker and good
at teaching. The trouble with Hugo Pearl was simply that
he talked too much and hated sticking to the truth.

It was nearly impossible to bring up the name of any
celebrity Hugo Pearl wouldn't claim he knew. He was as
likely as not to tell some stories about his life that involved himself and one or two well-known women at the
same time.

Dave Lawlor was leader of the jeering section. "Sure,
chum, you know everybody."

"Well, it just happens that I do."

"You never would think that all those people came to
New Jersey."

"I'm not so far from the George Washington Bridge
out there, and I can drive into New York," Hugo said
defensively.

His work was starting to suffer on account of the razz-
ing treatment, and Ablett took it up with Dave Lawlor.
The sergeant sighed, being able to see Chris Ablett's
point, but he had the idea that Hugo Pearl should be
taught a lesson.

"For God's sake, Sergeant," Ablett complained, "we've

really got a war out here. That ought to be enough to keep all of us pretty damn busy."

"Yes, sir, but we have to fight it with people, and I'm raising one point about one person."

"Do you think Pearl ought to be transferred?"

"No, sir. He's a damn good worker. But I think he can be cured, like any other ham."

"How?"

Lawlor told him. Chris Ablett sighed. He didn't much like the idea, but if it would shut up Pearl and make Lawlor feel any better he was willing to let him go ahead with it.

Lawlor and Sergeant Pepper, who had been sent in as Overby's replacement, made a point of talking when they were within Hugo Pearl's earshot in the emergency dispensary near the base perimeter.

"Her's an important man," Lawlor was saying, as if he and Pepper had been in conversation for a little while.

"I know it," Pepper nodded. "Got a beautiful daughter, too, they tell me. Somebody I'd like to meet."

Hugo Pearl gave one of those revealing snickers that generally introduced one of his made-up stories.

Lawlor said tiredly, "I know, Pearl. You've met her. Isn't that right?"

"Well, I wouldn't want you fellows to think I'm stretching the truth," Pearl began.

"You, Pearly?" Lawlor looked astonished. "Never!"

"A blond girl, isn't she?" Pepper asked.

"You guys are trying to trap me," Pearl said. "As a matter of fact, she was a redhead when I knew her, and I knew her pretty well, too."

"How tall?"

"Oh, about yay high." Pearl held a hand up to center-chest. "Women are able to monkey with their height, too, you know. Unless you see them in bed. In this case, I did."

"And you know her father, too?"

"I met him when I called for her," Pearl said. "But I

don't know him real well. I'm not lying, fellows. If I was, I'd say me and him were real close."

"Do you think he'd remember you?"

"I wouldn't be surprised. After all, we did do a little talking."

Pepper burst out, "You don't even know who it is, Pearly. You just started jabbering because you wanted a chance to put one over on us."

"I know who you're talking about, and don't ask me to tell you, either. I don't want to play childish games."

Pepper, not having expected that Hugo Pearl could lie his way out of what had seemed like a foolproof trap, turned to Dave Lawlor.

Then Lawlor had his great idea. "I'm glad he'd remember you," Lawlor said, "because you'll be seeing him today."

That made Pearl jump as if he'd been kicked from behind. "What? What do you mean?"

"Why, Colonel Esterbrook is coming out with the new captain, you know," Lawlor said jovially. "You and the colonel can have a little talk about old times."

"Sure," Pepper said cheerfully. "And you've been such a good friend of his daughter."

"Wait a minute," Pearl said quickly. "You weren't talking about Colonel Esterbrook to begin with."

"Sure we were."

"Then you don't know his daughter after all?" Lawlor asked. "And you don't know him?"

Pearl couldn't stand admitting that he wasn't a friend of important people, or at the very least an acquaintance. He hesitated.

Lawlor said, "In that case, we'll let you alone with him when the colonel gets here. It would be a shame to keep two old pals away from each other."

"Look, fellows—" Pearl began.

"Only too glad to do you a favor." Lawlor was grinning from ear to ear. "We'll arrange everything."

It was a sick-looking Hugo Pearl who watched Colonel

189

Esterbrook's chopper land in the clearing at the base. The colonel, a hearty-looking Regular Army type, stepped out of the chopper and gestured at another man, then hurried to the orderly room. The man who followed Esterbrook out of the chopper was young and solemn-looking. He glanced around him as if examining a new home he had just moved into.

The new captain's name was Alexander Birrell, and he had fought the Cong and the NVA troops up and down the country. He was at least a year or two younger than Lawlor, the team sergeant saw as he and Ablett joined the newcomers in the orderly room for a briefing, and he didn't do much talking. He asked sensible questions, though, and Lawlor mentally put down a check mark of approval next to the new captain's name.

Ablett did most of the talking, being the base's ranking U.S. officer as of a few moments ago and most familiar with the setup.

"Charlie and the NVA have been hitting pretty hard lately," Ablett said. "They know that if they can wipe us out, the NVA can infiltrate a damn sight easier than now, and they're making a push to do it along with NVA help that gets bigger all the time."

Birrell nodded and said, "I'll want to inspect the camp as soon as possible."

"Yes, sir," Ablett said. "We'll all go."

Lawlor cleared his throat. "One small point, sir. It's a distraction, but the men are interested." He launched into an account of the trap that had accidentally been evolved for Hugo Pearl.

"I don't have a daughter," the colonel said when Lawlor was finished, "and I'll take some pleasure in letting your Sergeant Pearl know about that. I may even threaten to put him up on charges. By God, yes! I haven't chewed out anybody for a whole Goddamn day."

The inspection went smoothly, Birrell only asking a few questions and those the important ones. He must have been briefed pretty well in advance about his counterpart, Dac Hee Quang, so he asked very few questions

190

about the Vietnamese captain. Quang joined the inspection party at the halfway point and looked a little surprised to meet somebody who talked even less than he himself did.

Hugo Pearl was helping Jerry Garfine take a radio to pieces when the inspection party reached them. Most of the A team members were close by and could hear what might be a good chewing-out that was long overdue. Pearl and Garfine were told that they could stand at ease.

"This is Captain Birrell," Ablett said. "He'll be in charge from now on. Anything wrong, Pearl?"

Hugo Pearl glanced at the colonel and looked miserable. He couldn't seem to stop swallowing, and he had to wipe his mouth every minute or so.

"Colonel," Ablett said to Esterbrook, "you remember Sergeant Pearl, don't you?"

"Never saw the man before in my life," Esterbrook said with relish.

Lawlor said, "I had understood from Sergeant Pearl that he was well acquainted with you and your daughter."

"I've got no daughter." The colonel scowled ferociously. "Have you been spreading lies about me, Sergeant?"

"No, sir." Pearl swallowed. "There was some misunderstanding on Sergeant Lawlor's part, I'm afraid."

"Well, if I hear of you telling lies about me and my family, you'll definitely go up on charges. Is that clear?"

"Absolutely, sir."

Hugo Pearl was wiping his face with a handkerchief when most of the inspection party went on. Birrell, who didn't seem to have taken any serious notice of what had been happening, explained the matter in careful detail to the puzzled but polite Quang. His grip on even as trivial a point as that one was so strong and clear that Lawlor was impressed by the new captain all over again. He felt sure he was going to like Birrell.

If Lawlor and the rest of the men had been smart enough to leave the matter of Pearl's dressing down strictly alone, Hugo Pearl might have behaved himself from then

191

on. But Lawlor and Garfine did choose to have a laugh over it before catching forty winks one night. Pearl, of course, could hear everything they said.

"I never saw anybody so embarrassed like our chum over there," Garfine said.

Lawlor went into a fit of laughing at the very recollection.

Pearl said, "Well, you fellows have to remember that I made a slight mistake."

"You sure did."

"I thought I heard you mention the colonel's first name when you were talking about it, and afterward I—well, I couldn't tell you the whole truth."

"Who? Me and Dan Pepper didn't mention no name at all when we started to talk, and only then I decided to stick you into claiming the colonel was a buddy of yours."

"But that isn't what I thought I heard," Hugo Pearl said softly. "I admit I made a mistake."

Garfine warned, "He's going to pull a fast one, Dave. Watch out!"

"The colonel's first name is Harold, you know—that is, Harry, which is what I heard you say. But the colonel has got a brother named Lawrence, and naturally he's called Larry. You know the way brothers are, sometimes. They'd think it was funny to be called Harry and Larry."

"He's lying," Garfine said. "It's almost a pleasure to hear him because he's so good at it, but we should never have opened our traps after the colonel got through with him."

Lawlor nodded morosely. "Forget the whole thing, Pearl. We'll shut up if you will."

"You have to understand," Pearl said gravely. "I don't want the men on my team thinking I'm a liar, so I must explain what really happened. Larry Esterbrook is the one with the daughter, and I got to know her real well. *Larry* Esterbrook, this is."

Dan Pepper put in, "We're not outside, but it's snowing indoors."

192

Lawlor asked, "Why didn't you tell all this to the colonel when he was saying he'd cut off your nuts and pickle them?"

"I couldn't do that." Pearl looked modest. "I wasn't going to say how well I knew his niece. It wouldn't be polite, and besides that—"

"All right, all right," Lawlor said decisively. "You say the colonel's got a brother named Lawrence and a pretty niece, too. And the niece's name?"

"Scarlett. A real nice girl."

"I noticed you were reading *Gone with the Wind* a few days ago," Garfine said. "Is it possible you got the name Scarlett from there?"

"It's a coincidence," Pearl said glibly.

"Okay, then, buddy. Next time the colonel comes around to look us over, you won't mind if we ask him about his brother and niece and tell him you're a boy-friend of his niece's?"

"Don't do that." Hugo Pearl made believe he was worried for his friends, leaning forward and saying quickly, "Don't ever do that. The colonel gets excited pretty easily, and he's liable to give you a hard time if you even mention his brother."

"Give *you* a hard time, Hugo."

"No, you don't understand. I can't let you have all the details, but that brother is the black sheep of the colonel's family. He's been in prison more than once."

Dan Pepper said exultantly, "When Esterbrook hears this, Hugo, you really will get your nuts pickled."

"How can we ask, though?" Lawlor snapped. "Suppose the one-in-a-million shot comes off and what he's saying is true?"

"*Him?*"

"I'm not saying he's on the square, I'm just saying suppose he is for once."

"I'll take the chance and ask Esterbrook."

"And then this fink will say he was misunderstood and you'll be on charges."

"Goddamn, can't we win out at all?"

"Shut up all of you," Lawlor shouted.

From then on, Hugo Pearl was every bit as impossible as he had been up till then. The other men simply had to grit their teeth or call him a liar when he talked about the colonel's niece, who turned out to be a girl of enormous sexual versatility—at least the way Pearl told it. When he was challenged he would simply smile and say, "Talk to the colonel—he knows about her."

It was a shame nobody could bring himself to strangle Hugo Pearl. He happened to be a damned good man at his job, and no replacement was likely to be up to his standard.

To get under Dan Pepper's hide was much easier, but nobody wanted to. Pepper was a tall, rangy Californian whose father owned a gas station near Anaheim. He was hoping to make the army his career, and he had a pretty good chance of doing it if he survived this hitch.

What hung up Pepper and nearly turned him into a nervous wreck was a casual word or two from Marty Bland, of all people. Dan Pepper had come through a patrol in which only four men survived out of twenty-one, and he had missed death over a dozen times by his own count.

"You're lucky," Marty Bland said. "That's all there is to it. Just lucky."

There was something about being called lucky that got Pepper all bothered. It was like saying that he hadn't made it because of anything he had done and that every skill he had worked so hard to acquire wasn't necessary. Some supernatural mixup had helped him, and nothing else. And if luck was what he had, then luck could fade away and then he'd get reamed on his next time out.

From then on, Dan Pepper started checking to see if he was really lucky or careful instead. He managed to survive an ambush when his Viet counterpart bought it, but fourteen other guys did that, too. He just missed a mine that knocked off three men, but so did another fellow who was even closer to it. And one time, when sniper fire opened up on him while he was driving and he actually had the steering wheel shot out of his hands, he was able to prevent crashing the jeep and to get out of the car and use it as a shield. The sniper got away, but Pepper lived to tell the tale and build up his reputation for luck.

Pepper, in fact, was as jittery as a bride. It did him no good to find out that he was considered the team's lucky token, that for him to go on a mission was considered a sure sign that there was some chance of getting back in one piece.

It was nearly as bad for his nerves when he was refused entry into a dice game because he was just too damn lucky. Dave Lawlor offered him ten p-notes to blow on the dice before he made a pass, but Pepper cursed everybody in sight and stalked away from that game.

It was no surprise to find out that the new captain was a little leery of him too and made a point of looking him up and down the first time they got together by themselves. Birrell, not being much of a talker, kept any thoughts on the other side of his thin lips.

"You've got demo training?" Birrell asked.

"Yes, sir."

"Good. It'll come in handy tonight."

"Sir?"

"We're leading a mission back of the enemy lines to give the NVA boys a hard time. You're invited to come along."

"Yes, sir."

"In fact, I finally got it out of Bland that if you're with it, the mission can't fail."

"That's just a joke among the men, sir, about my being lucky."

"Army people don't consider good luck or bad to be any sort of a joke, as you must be aware."

"Yes, sir."

"Very well, then. You'll meet me and Bland and the Viet counterparts here at eighteen hundred. That'll be all."

Pepper left and got busy on his day's work, which

didn't give him too much trouble. He had noticed a long time ago that just before a really dangerous mission other problems smoothed themselves out as if to give a man more time to worry about the danger ahead.

Lieutenant Ablett told him at one point that a shipment of beer had come in and suggested that Pepper load himself up with a little of the stuff before setting out for the night.

"Thanks, Lieutenant. I'll do that."

"Fine." Ablett laughed self-consciously. "I was going to wish you good luck, but in your case that's pretty much unnecessary, isn't it?"

Pepper winced, but he said, "An extra wish can't do any harm, sir."

"I suppose you're right, Sergeant. Good luck."

"Thank you, sir."

Beer cans were stacked up from the floor to a point parallel with Pepper's shoulders, as the sergeant found out when he reached the PX tent. He grabbed a can, paid for it, then opened the damn thing and drank a little of it.

He was suddenly aware of a burning sensation in his mouth, and he managed to spit out a little of the stuff, at least.

"Loaded," he called out to Marty Bland, who was opening a can with thumb and forefinger. "Mine is loaded."

That was what he started to say, but the words wouldn't come. Instead, Pepper was very well aware that liquid was pouring out of his mouth and that it wasn't beer.

Marty ran to fetch Sid Wheeler. The medic worked long and hard with Pepper, trying to stem the flow of blood. It took time and patience and cunning. When the job was done in part and Pepper lay on the dispensary table, still gasping at remembered agony, Wheeler said, "The stomach pump worked and so did the other emergency measures, so you're okay."

Pepper couldn't talk.

"How Charlie got to the beer I'll never know," Wheeler

said glumly. "I heard about somebody who opened up a can and found himself on the other end of a popping grenade. You're just lucky, as usual."

Pepper pointed to his swollen and painful mouth and gums in hopes of showing Wheeler what a lie it was to call him lucky.

"You've got a little inconvenience, Dan, but you won't be going on no mission tonight. I'll have to make the scene instead of you."

Pepper put out a hand, offering to shake with Wheeler and wish him luck. Sid Wheeler smiled affably and took it.

"Well, Dan, you're the one who's got a corner on the luck market. See you when I get back. When and if, of course."

Pepper never knew or cared how he was able to get any sleep that night. Every so often, people would walk overhead and the wooden beams in the dugout dispensary would shake like false teeth in a glass, but nothing happened. The Cong and the NVA ran one of their usual night attacks, too, but Pepper knew he was out of it for the night. He hoped that he'd be able to talk pretty soon, that he wouldn't have to go to any Goddamn hospital.

It was daylight when Pepper woke up and saw a flood of light at the dispensary entrance. He didn't realize that he'd been awakened by somebody coming in, but he heard the steps slurring against the dirt and blinked his eyes again and again before he made out Sid Wheeler and Marty Bland.

The medic checked him over before anything else happened. "You'll be okay in a little while," he decided. "A hospital trip won't do you any harm in case there's something I missed. I'd advise you to keep your trap shut, but you'll be okay, Lucky."

He said that word as if he meant it to be set off by quote marks on either side. Pepper looked startled.

"You really missed a ball," Marty Bland said. "The

197

real goods, as far as missions go. Number one—no casualties. Not even a mosquito bite. How's that for a dangerous mission behind enemy lines?"

"Number two," Wheeler went on, grinning, "we got to the NVA headquarters and found us a raft of forged U.S. money. If you think we aren't going to get some sort of an award for turning the stuff in, then you don't know Uncle Sam. By the way, we also smashed the press that was faking the stuff, and faking p-notes into the bargain.

"The NVA had some wine, and we took that," Wheeler said. "We took his girls, too. There were four damn attractive broads over in that place, and they said they'd play ball if we let 'em live. So we took turns. The girls didn't mind, and we had us a great time.

"Another thing. We managed to plant a few calling cards where the NVA won't find 'em until it comes time for the damn things to blow up. The girls came away with us because we convinced 'em they'd be better off at Tam Hung. And they really will be. Every man at the base will see to that."

Sid Wheeler chuckled. "You really missed the mission of a lifetime, Lucky," he said, with that same pause before and after the last word. "You had to become a casualty beforehand, just like any other guy might. And here we figured you were infallible."

Marty Bland said, "The luck tripped you up for sure, Pep, and you're just as much of a shlubbo as the rest of us."

Pepper smiled as best he could. He wasn't feeling in such good condition, heaven knew, but he realized he'd got his friends back, and that alone was enough to make him happy.

"You'll be all right in a day or so," Sid Wheeler said to him before leaving. "Get yourself some more shut-eye. It can't do you any harm, Lucky."

Ken Hubbard was wondering whether the hut occupied in the village by Co See and her children wouldn't be the ideal spot for a new schoolhouse. He stood in front

198

of the hut, brooding about it, and then decided to talk to the woman and see if she would move into the hut that had been used by Tran Cao Cha before the old man's recent death. That hut would be fixed up and made to look like new, if Co See went along with his idea. The need for it was brought on because the village mothers wouldn't send their children to a hut that had been lived in by a man who'd lost his mind.

He knocked on the door and nearly fell back in surprise when it was opened by Ha Binh. Sunlight made the girl's face look several shades whiter than he was used to seeing it.

She closed the door on the hut and stood outside with him.

"I returned by airplane," she said, probably the only villager ever to have flown and well aware of it. "I had to come back."

"I'm sorry you did. The Vietcong and the North Vietnamese are becoming much more active. They do things that they wouldn't otherwise have done."

Ha Binh shrugged. "I hope that I shall survive."

"I hope so too, Ha Binh." He paused, then told her why he had come and what he wanted from Co See.

Ha Binh said consideringly, "You cannot ask Co See to bring up her children in a house where a man lost his mind."

"She'd have a much better home."

"But the memories would be too heavy," Ha Binh said quickly. "I will advise her against it."

Ken winced. In that case he might just as well say goodbye to the best idea he'd had in quite a while. Building a new schoolhouse for the native kids would take time and effort that he and the other men ought to be giving toward chasing the Cong and the NVA out of their holes.

He smiled down at her and turned to go, not being able to guess that he'd never again see Ha Binh on her feet.

He had taken five steps, when he heard small-arms fire

behind him. Swiftly he turned, seeing a small, furious gunman in black pajamas. He was standing near the hut that had previously been used by Tran Cao Cha, using the open door as a shield.

Ken pulled the spoon out of a grenade and threw it. The earth under him shook violently, but only for a few seconds. It was all over when he saw the hut door off its hinges and the Cong, or whatever might be left of him, motionless under big chunks of door.

At last his eyes swept the street as he searched for Ha Binh. She lay on her stomach, face down in the mud. He hurried over and turned her around, telling himself that he had never said to her that he loved her and wanted to marry her and take her back with him to the hill country of Kentucky. He had been scared. He'd got the impression that a marriage between them could never work, but he'd been wrong. He had to have been—

She was dead. There couldn't be any mistake about that. He wasn't twenty-four years old yet, but he had seen death often enough.

Ha Binh had taken a bullet aimed at him, just as her late husband had done. Now the two of them were dead and Ken Hubbard was alive—and what the hell was he doing with his life? What use was it to himself or to other people?

When he stood up, hard lines had formed in his youthful face. He would go into the hut and tell Co See what was on his mind and try to get cooperation for moving her while he located the village schoolhouse in this hut. He would have to get some men to help him fix both huts, but that could be managed. Co See was likely to go along with what Ken wanted, since it was going to make conditions better for her and for so many others, as well. The last obstacle to getting Co See's agreement had been—

Ken Hubbard blinked a few times, shook his head violently as if he wanted to clear his thoughts away, and then knocked on Co See's door. . . .

200

Dave Lawlor demanded, "What in hell do you mean, gone?"

"I can't help it." Jerry Garfine looked everywhere around the camp except at Dave Lawlor's red face. "Do you think I wanted anything should happen to him?"

"Well, I'll tell you this much, Sergeant Garfine—if Marty Bland is in any sort of trouble, God help *you!*"

"He disappeared, I'm telling you. One minute we were on patrol, and the next minute he was gone. God knows we looked around, but there wasn't any trace of him."

Lawlor scratched his jaw furiously. "You better show me where it happened, Jerry."

"The two of us going out alone? Well, I'll do it if you want."

"All right, kid." Lawlor nearly smiled. "I'm sorry if I blew my top. Now let's get Marty back."

They didn't have to go out alone. Marty's Viet counterpart, Thanh Van Nhu, liked Marty as much as everybody else in the camp did, and he asked if he could go along. Some other Viets asked for permission too. All in all, twelve men went out to find Marty Bland.

The men were only a quarter of the way to their destination, by Jerry Garfine's guess, when they came across Marty. For a minute, every last one of them wished he had stayed back at base.

Marty was hanging from a banyan tree. Dirty rope had been looped under his thin neck. His narrow face was white and contorted. There wasn't a stitch of clothing on him, and it was plain that he had been repeatedly beaten and bayoneted.

Jerry Garfine said tautly, "What a hell of a way to reform a country!"

"One of the nicest guys I ever knew," Lawlor said, his voice becoming thick. "He didn't deserve that."

"Let's get him off there."

Dave Lawlor started to nod but then he stopped himself and said, "Hold it a minute, Jerry."

"What's wrong?"

201

"We'd better pull back and throw a rock at—at what's left."

Jerry Garfine's face was gray. "I know he wouldn't feel anything, but I can't do that."

"I will, then. Just get the hell back, all of you."

The men obeyed Jerry's gestures. Lawlor found a rock and threw it at the dead body. The earth shivered under him as the trap blew up, scattering pieces to the winds. If they hadn't heard the noise of bombs blowing up several hundred times in the past few months, the sound might have deafened every man on the mission. As it was, even Dave Lawlor had to put both hands to his ears.

"Let's get back to base," Lawlor said, when he could make himself understood again. "There isn't enough of Marty left to take with us."

"Bastards," Garfine said, choked with anger. "Miserable bastards."

Lawlor, who might have been expected to curse a blue streak, was calm while they were all in the jungle and without any protection except what they could manage for themselves.

But he made up for it when they got back to the base, telling the other men what had happened and then going to make a report to Captain Birrell.

Birrell was at the CP leafing through carbon copies of Matt Colbert's Monthly Operations Summary Reports. He looked up, jaw thrust out.

Lawlor made his report in the fewest possible words, then waited for the roof to fall in on him.

Birrell said, "I've been told that Sergeant Bland was a friend of everybody's as well as a good man on the job. I understand the feeling that prompted you to go out there with the others. I sympathize with it as a man, but not as your commanding officer. You allowed yourself to put eleven people in jeopardy."

"Everybody volunteered to go, sir."

"If somebody volunteers to stick his head in a lion's mouth the fact remains that he's in jeopardy," Birrell

202

said, lips drawn tight with anger. "You could all have been ambushed, and we can't spare any of you. I'm under the impression that the NVA is planning an all-out fight around the base, and we'll need every man to bleed him real good."

"Yes, sir."

"I want to be notified next time you think about taking a little jaunt off-base," Birrell said levelly, bringing a flush of anger up along Lawlor's parchment-colored cheeks. "Dismissed, Team Master Sergeant Lawlor. Dismissed."

The boy squirmed in Sid Wheeler's grasp. He wasn't more than twelve years old, dark-faced and scrawny. He probably hadn't ever taken a bath in his life.

Wheeler had caught him trying to steal a grenade from the helmet he had put down before starting one of his regular sick calls. He had kept the boy at his side till the sick call was finished, then turned to him and cuffed him.

"If you had killed me, some of your own people would have died," he said. "Do you understand that?"

The boy said nothing.

Wheeler cold-bloodedly applied pressure to the boy's stomach. The boy whimpered, then cried.

"I asked if you understand that."

"Y-yes."

"Good. If you kill me, you kill your own people in this village, or at least some of them. I would die swiftly, but they would die in pain. Do you understand that, too?"

"Yes."

"Better and better. I take it that you have seen what dead bodies look like."

"Yes."

"It disgusts me that you should want to add even one more to the total," Wheeler said. He stepped back and away from the boy. "If I hear of any other mischief that you do, I shall kill you with my bare hands. Is that clear?"

"Yes."

"And you can believe me when I say so," Wheeler said grimly. "I am not telling you a grandmother tale."

"I understand."

"Then go."

The boy blinked incredulously. "You are letting me leave?"

"Ask no questions."

The boy nodded. "You will shoot me in the back. I have heard of that American trick."

Wheeler made as if to kick the boy, but he darted out of reach and ran to the door. He opened it, then turned slowly to see the tired medic not aiming a gun at him but only making a check on the contents of his medic bag.

That was when the boy turned childish again. He had tried to kill Wheeler, but now he couldn't show defiance in any other way except to stick out his tongue at the colored medic. He did it and shut the door after him.

It opened again on Dan Pepper, who had been working around the base perimeter and decided he could use a few aspirins because he felt a cold coming on.

"That little kid ought to take a bath," Pepper said mildly. He talked slowly ever since getting back from the hospital at Pleiku. There was a small gash half the size of a ten-cent piece at the left of his upper lip.

"That kid ought to have some brains, too," Wheeler muttered. "I'll be damned if he didn't try to snatch a grenade out of my hat while I was working."

"And you let him go?"

"I let him sit through the medical session and then scared the shit out of him. What was I supposed to do to the kid, shoot him?"

"Why not?" Pepper asked. "He'd do it to you. How do I know who loaded that beer and almost sent me six feet under?"

"A kid of twelve doesn't know a damn thing."

"He knows enough to kill," Pepper said. "If I were you, Sid, I'd hope like hell that he doesn't try his tricks

204

on somebody else. He might make it next time, thanks to his having been given another chance."

Wheeler brushed that off with a few light words, but when he got back to base himself he found out that Pepper had talked about what had happened. He got a chewing out from the team master sergeant, and Lawlor couldn't be stopped once he was really underway. Wheeler knew that the other men were po'd about what he'd done when he saw that even the mild-mannered Jerry Garfine didn't talk to him as much as usual.

It was only a matter of time before the captain would have a few words to say, and Birrell called him over when the night guard was getting started. Birrell sat on a rock and invited Wheeler to sit on a smaller one that faced him. The captain kept quiet at first, probably supposing that Wheeler would want to blurt out some apology or excuse and put himself at a disadvantage from the start. Sid Wheeler kept his mouth shut, though.

Finally Alec Birrell said, "I hear you had a run-in with a young kid who tried to knock you off."

"He tried to steal one of my grenades, and I suppose he'd have tried to kill me with it, sir."

"Would you know the boy again?"

Wheeler said tautly, "I know his father by name, so I'm sure I could get hold of the kid any time."

"You know his father? I wasn't told that."

Wheeler was going to say that Dan Pepper didn't know everything but stopped himself.

Birrell asked, "Have you talked to the father?"

"No, sir, I haven't."

"We'll both do it tomorrow," Birrell decided. "I'll look the kid up and down myself, and if I don't like what I see, then I'll have to . . ."

Wheeler asked, "You'll have to kill him?"

"I don't want to risk one man's life because of a possible enemy in the gates."

"He's just a twelve-year-old kid, sir, and he doesn't know his ass from a hole in the ground."

"He'd better find out fast," Birrell said. "If I decide you've made a bloop, Wheeler, I'll sheet you for it."

"Yes, sir."

The night passed reasonably well, with only some more probing actions from Charlie or his NVA buddies. There was more sniper fire than usual, though. Even Birrell, who had been at the base for only three days, noticed it.

"They're testing us, I think," he said at one point. And then, half-smiling at Wheeler, he added, "I hope that little twelve-year-old monster isn't out there and shooting."

"He isn't, sir."

It was midafternoon of the next day and unusually hot for late October, when Birrell and Wheeler got out of one of the base jeeps and went to the hut of a farmer who had been persuaded to make his home at Tam Hung. The ex-farmer, Thon Cho Mi, was a tall man with hard eyes and a sprig of mustache. He didn't invite the two army men into his hut but talked to them in front of the granary.

Thon heard Birrell out and said that his son was a stupid, misguided boy. He whistled for the twelve-year-old, whose name was Ngo, and the boy came running out to join his father. He paused when he saw Wheeler and Birrell but didn't run away from what looked like trouble.

Birrell watched him carefully as he came forward, eyes wide, lips pursed, hands at his sides.

"Well, lad," Birrell said, his own narrowed eyes never leaving the boy. "Are you a good student?"

The father shouted, "Speak!" because young Ngo couldn't bring himself to say one word.

He finally nodded.

"I know that you and this friend of ours"—Birrell pointed to Wheeler—"have had difficulties, but I hope that everything will be all right between you from now on."

Birrell wasn't used to talking so much, and he had to clear his throat afterward. The boy couldn't have said one word if he had known that his life might depend on it.

206

"You're a good boy," Birrell said, smiling. "You can go now, if your father wishes it."

"Yes, go," the father said sternly, "and embarrass me no more."

Instead of running the boy walked off, and he stopped when he was near his father's hut. Birrell and Thon said a few more words to each other, and then the father turned to a village friend and began talking to him about the chances of farming again in the near future.

Birrell, left with Wheeler, made his face look cheerful. "Smile and pretend we're talking about other things."

"Yes, sir," Wheeler said, obeying his superior as his lips strained in a smile. "What do you think of the boy, sir?"

"Not much."

"You wouldn't seriously want to kill him?"

"Well, put him under guard, perhaps, and arrange for his relocation. I couldn't be absolutely sure whether or not he was actively against us."

"If you have that done, sir, it's likely to make Thon and his friends pretty mad."

"Let it make them mad if it saves one life."

"Yes, sir," Wheeler said unhappily.

They started to walk between the houses. On the way past young Ngo, the boy shyly smiled at Wheeler.

"I think he wants to talk to me, sir."

"The boy? He's probably got another grenade in his hand by this time, a homemade job."

"In that case, sir, he'd have tried to kill both of us."

"Birrell's nod admitted that. "Do you want to risk your neck and talk with him?"

"He won't do me any hurt, sir." Wheeler smiled lightly. "I can tell him about Chieu Hoi."

Birrell didn't smile back at the reference to the Vietnamese program to settle defected Vietcong members in certain areas.

"Save the humor for another time," Birrell said. "You can talk to the boy if you want. I'll cover."

Wheeler turned and walked back toward the boy.

"Well, Ngo?" he asked. "What is it now?"

The boy said carefully, "I was hoping that you might be able to give me some chocolate."

Wheeler nodded grimly and took a bar of chocolate from one pocket. The boy didn't thank him.

"All right, Ngo," Wheeler said. "I stopped to give you a piece of chocolate and if anybody is looking on, then that's the only reason I stopped. Is there anything you want to tell me very quickly?"

"N-no," the boy said.

Wheeler looked at him for as much as another half a minute, then turned to go. As he was taking his first step away from him, the boy whispered, "They come at night."

Wheeler didn't move or turn back but stood and brushed at his uniform as if it had become dirty. His back was toward Ngo, protecting the boy in case some enemy was watching. He could see Birrell looking at him with no approval whatever.

"It happens tonight," the boy whispered. "Many will come. I know because the people in the village who are with them in spirit have told me so. You can still save yourself."

Wheeler couldn't show that he was touched by the boy's wanting to return a favor. He had to whirl around and shout at the boy, calling him half a dozen names that were considered as deadly insults. If any of young Ngo's Cong sympathizer friends heard that, it would convince them that the boy wasn't friendly toward Americans. He couldn't wink to show he hadn't meant a word of what he was saying, and the boy looked white-faced. Wheeler had to stalk away without telling the boy what he had just tried to do for him.

When he joined Birrell some ten feet off, the captain said accusingly, "You turned your back on him."

"Yes, sir, but for a good reason." He gave it, adding what the boy had said.

Birrell drew a deep breath. Wheeler, who was beginning to know what was on a superior officer's mind whether the man said so or not, felt sure he'd never get any other acknowledgment from Birrell that the captain had nearly made a mistake.

Eighteen

THE BATTLE OF TAM HUNG started small but was likely to get bigger in a little while. The enemy was making his strongest try yet to wipe out the base and its defenders so that North Vietnamese soldiers would be able to infiltrate more securely.

Alex Birrell was awakened just before dawn when a flare landed too close to him. He darted to the left automatically, slipping out of his black silk hammock and landing on one knee and one hand, just as he'd wanted to.

A bugle blew, and he saw a number of enemy charge against the camp wire at the outer perimeter. Three claymore mines thrown by Dave Lawlor and two Viets were enough to stop that particular charge, most of that wave of enemy reeling back filled with buckshot.

The stutter of machine-gun fire was closer than any of the men at base wanted it to be. Dac Hee Quang, having been on the alert for several hours now, had made his plans. He sent one of his best men out with a twelve-gauge shotgun. The man, whose name was Than Che Ho, had to crawl out to a point some seventy-five yards from the outer perimeter, and a single shotgun blast did the trick when he got there. He was shot in the back as he was crawling back to base, but threw his twelve-gauge into a stream so it wouldn't fall into enemy hands. Before he was found the enemy had shot his head off and bayoneted the body.

Jerry Garfine was sitting at his radio equipment taking Quang's orders in calling for air strikes. The air people had been alerted last night, and fighter-bombers appeared in the sky almost as soon as called for, pounding the attackers with napalm. When the planes drew back, the enemy started his mortar attack. The first shell killed four CIDG men, who were caught before they could duck for cover.

Dave Lawlor was trying to spot the place where mortar fire was coming from. When he thought he had seen it, just over the hill, he sank down to one knee and grabbed for an M-79 grenade launcher. There was a pink flash as a grenade spring-loaded with steel barbs sped away from the projectile. He could see it explode, but he had to squint his eyes to make it out. The mortar fire kept on.

"You missed the bastard," Benson muttered. He was a psych warfare man from Scottsdale, Arizona, and his job took him out of the base camp as often as it kept him inside.

"Watch this," Dave Lawlor muttered, reloading from a cannister with double-O buckshot that would cut down anything some twenty feet in front of him. "A little close-in work."

Four enemy had been climbing the wire, but they fell dead at one burst from the launcher.

The mortar fire was still keeping up, killing wherever it hit.

Quang called for another air strike, this time closer than the previous ones had been. The noise was so loud that nothing could be done while the strike went forward, and the enemy could still move around singly.

One soldier pinned Hubbard down for a while. Ken, keeping himself from running at the bastard, managed to crawl into one of the heavy-weapon holes and get himself an M-60. It was easier to get the machine gun than the bullet belt, and he had to wait around till the supply man could issue him one. When he looked out again, the enemy soldier was flat on the ground and crawling slowly toward the CP. There was a dead CIDG next to him, and Ken supposed that the enemy crawling away had done that job.

Planting the M-60 on its snake-high bipod, Ken fired. The M-60 never jumped when it was in use, as so many guns did, and Ken was able to aim with consistent care. That one dead enemy was weighted down with fourteen bullet holes by the time Ken stopped shooting.

Jerry Garfine would wait till there was a pause in the flow of radio messages, then take an M-16, step into the open air, glance toward the outer perimeter, spray a short burst of rifle fire, and run back in again.

Birrell and Quang were pacing the communications room, each man trying to think clearly.

"The enemy is making quite a gamble on this attack," Quang said, underlining the obvious is a way that Birrell would never have done. "He has to be countered."

"Air strikes can't do the job alone," Birrell said. "More troops may be necessary."

Quang nodded. Birrell gave Garfine the signal to send for troops. The return message was simply that two battalions of Vietnamese were on the way. Birrell looked a little more at ease. Quang glared at everybody, as if he wanted nothing more than to get hold of Garfine's M-16 and run outside and fight next to the men he was commanding. Birrell sympathized with him, heaven knew, but couldn't bring himself to say so.

It was Quang, of course, who brought the difficulty out and made himself plain. "To be in charge is more difficult than to fight," he said. "Fighting is simple. Even dying can be simple. Hoping to make sense out of what goes on out there and carry the responsibility for so many lives, that is difficult. Truly that is difficult."

Birrell, embarrassed by the emotional tone of Quang's voice, was able only to nod. Then he looked away promptly and started studying a map.

He heard Quang's voice again, gently sardonic. "The captain busies himself with the head rather than the heart."

Half an hour of agony went past before Garfine could communicate the bad news from Batcat, the B team headquarters.

"Two battalions were helicoptered down at the enemy's

212

right, but there's more enemy outside than anybody guessed, and the two battalions are pinned down."

Quang swore. Birrell asked softly, "Are more men on the way?"

"Yes, sir, but it'll take time for them to get here."

"What about air strikes?"

"Air is flying to help the others, too, so they can't cover the camp and the battalions."

"How far off are the battalions?"

"They're dug in about five miles from here, sir, according to Batcat."

A scream could be heard from the emergency dispensary, where Sid Wheeler was having his hands full. Fourteen men had been dragged in. They'd have to be handled somehow, and Wheeler swiftly looked over each man to decide whose life he couldn't save and whose would have to be practically thrown out because there was no time to try to help him.

Fred Jensen, who'd had some medic cross-training, came in for a few minutes to help, but he had to run out again.

Wheeler suddenly heard himself shouting, "Where's the Goddamn morphine? *Where is it?*"

His hands shook with anger. For the first time since getting into Special Forces, Wheeler lost every trace of self-control.

There was a med emergency kit over in his tent, and he decided he was damn right well going to get the stuff. He picked up an M-16 and ran out of the dispensary toward the tent he shared with the other Americans. He cut a zigzag path in spite of the hellish sounds on all sides of him and was somehow able to keep from tripping over such obstructions as dead men and discarded weapons on every side. He ran to his tent, got the emergency kit, and started back. He was halfway to the emergency dispensary, when an enemy soldier loomed in front of him. There was nothing to be done except fight for passage.

He dropped the medical bag for which he had risked

his life and, using the M-16 as a bludgeon, started to hit the enemy with the gun stock. The enemy, a slim and fierce youth who carried a knife, suddenly buried the tip of his knife in the stock. The plastic butt of the M-16 shattered, leaving each man without a weapon as far as Sid Wheeler could see.

Wheeler kicked the enemy soldier in the stomach, and when the soldier doubled up he knocked him unconscious with a karate chop against the back of the neck. He thought he had killed the boy and wondered for a frantic moment how he had ever been able to get used to the routine of killing and saving, killing and saving.

Weaponless now, he picked up the bag and ran toward the dispensary. A slight young enemy soldier cut him down before he could do anything more than duck and try to change direction. Wheeler felt considerable pressure in his nose as he slid into the dirt, and he never knew anything else.

The enemy soldier reached for the emergency medical kit bag with its pain-relieving supplies. The kit didn't have any weapons in it, so the soldier grunted and threw the kit away from him.

Dan Pepper was using an M-16 too, but with more luck on his side at the moment. He was sprawled down in a hole near the perimeter and firing short bursts. He had carried four hundred and fifty rounds into the battle with him, and he felt pretty sure he had accounted for eight or nine enemy at least. He had been scatter-firing as a rule, but in order to get good aim he had to raise his head and chest. It worked for him and his kill-number was on the way up, but some enemy spotted him and a grenade missed him by less than a yard.

The enemy raised himself, Pepper saw, looking out. He anchored himself once again, fired pointblank at the grenade, and dropped back so that he could cover his head. Fragments of that enemy were probably scattered all over camp.

Even above the noise of gunfire men could be heard

shouting for a med aid team. Jensen, who hated medic work, had taken the job over, and that was a sure sign to the others that Sid Wheeler was KIA.

Hugo Pearl was directing return fire from one of the dugouts when a shell dropped short. It killed the rest of his crew, but Pearl had a lucky break and only lost his right eye. He staggered into the dispensary, somehow avoiding enemy marauders and not realizing that three enemy were following him.

As he got into the dispensary the three enemy acted. They hurried in, ignoring the groans of pain and shock from the men. Swiftly and silently they bayoneted every wounded man. Most of them cried out, but when they did that another bayonet wound to the same body was sure to follow. Pearl looked around wildly, hoping to find the door. As he took one step toward it, a bayonet wound opened in his back. He whirled and fell. The stench of blood, mixed with the smell of dirt and fresh bandages, was everywhere, and Pearl wished he was dead too, instead of being so badly wounded.

Above the dispensary and at ground level, a number of enemy came running into the base camp, screaming as they charged. The pressure of running footsteps against the shaky logs that had always kept a cave-in from happening was too much for them now, and the logs fell. The three enemy were battered to death. Hugo Pearl could hear their groans as they dropped, one above him. Pearl never knew how he had been able to survive this much, but he didn't survive for long. Six days afterward at the hospital in Pleiku, he suddenly shouted, "I can see again—I can see out of both eyes"; then he died.

Simon Lessner was one of the team replacements who'd had just about enough time to get acquainted with the other men on this A team. He had stopped to burn a leech off himself with a cigarette when he saw one of the enemy running toward him.

Lessner didn't hesitate but picked up his M-16 and started firing. The enemy, a small youngster with a knife

215

between his teeth, survived three bullets but shut his eyes on the fourth and crumpled up. Lessner fired two more bullets into the boy's head in order to make sure that the boy wouldn't bother anybody else again. He always hated to do that, but he'd never hate it again. Those two bullets saved his life, as it happened, and not on account of the dead boy, either.

Every time an M-16 is fired, whether it's at the clip of 70 rounds a minute or just a shot snapped off into the darkness in the hope of finding an enemy, it's 5.56-millimeter cartridge casings pop upward and hang in the air for a second or so. Lessner's casings as he swiveled the gun around had hit an approaching enemy across the eyes, and the enemy called out with shock.

There was enough time for Lessner to raise the gun and fire it twice, then fire twice more at the dead man's head. He'd never again think twice about doing that.

Douglas Dill, another of the new replacements, was working an M-60 machine gun for everything he could get out of it. When the gun got overheated he reached for an M-16, but there wasn't a single bullet in the damn thing. He started to realize that if some enemy came after him he wouldn't be able to defend himself—not unless he had a chance to use his bare hands, and that didn't seem likely.

A mortar shell came roaring down not far away. Dill covered his head, then felt somebody else in the hole with him. When the shell burst was over he and the other soldier looked up and faced each other for the first time. The other was a Vietnamese, small and with burning dark eyes.

"You have no weapon," the other soldier said.

Dill was put on the alert by that oddly rising and mocking inflection. He gestured toward the machine gun.

"If the weapon could be used, you would be doing so," the other soldier pointed out.

The same inflection of mockery laced with fear made Dill ask the other soldier, "Are you from North Vietnam?"

Silence.

216

"And you wear the uniform of a South Vietnamese soldier?" Dill straightened up. The other man was carrying a knife, two grenades, and a hand gun, as well as a standard-issue M-16. "Why do you tell me that you're an infiltrator?"

He wished he was more sharp when it came to reading faces. The soldier was in the grip of some strong feeling, but Dill couldn't guess what it was. The glowing eyes, the sweaty hands, the inability to move, all hinted that the soldier was scared out of his wits.

"Is this your first mission?"

"Yes."

Douglas Dill did something he'd never in a million years have thought was in him. He said, "Why don't you stay here?"

The other soldier looked confused.

"You stay here for a while, and when a little time has gone past you go back to your side and say you killed a few of ours. You'll be a hero."

The soldier frowned. "But you'll do something to me, won't you?"

"Leave us alone, and we'll do the same to you." Dill stared. "How old are you?"

"Fifteen. I seem much older."

"You might never actually make it, though." Afterward it would surprise Dill to think he could've held a conversation in the teeth of a seesawing life-and-death battle, with bombs dropping not too far away. He must've had to raise his voice, but he never remembered that. "Were you drafted?"

"Of course."

"What sort of work do you plan to do when the war is finished?"

"To be a farmer, like my father was." The boy shivered. "Something could happen here."

"It sure could." Dill wiped his nose with the back of a hand. "You've got a clear run over to the dispensary. It ought to be safe for you over there."

"But I have no wound," the boy protested.

217

"Well, I think the dispensary is the safest spot, and that's the only advice I can give you." Dill never knew what made him say, "I wish I could do better."

The boy flashed him a look of gratitude, then climbed out of the hole and started running toward the dispensary. Dill fingered his M-60, which wasn't overheated any longer, but decided against doing the kid any harm.

It was a North Vietnamese soldier who cut the infiltrator down, bayoneting the boy as he was on the move. Dill saw the boy's hands rise pleadingly in the air. He fell and didn't stir.

With his machine gun, Dill made short work of the enemy soldier and then felt glad the son of a bitch was dead. The kid-killing son of a bitch.

Dave Lawlor was working an M-60 too. He was in a hole at a point where he could shout across to his new Viet counterpart, who was only about half Lawlor's size but didn't seem to care any more than Lawlor whether he came out of the day's fighting or not.

"See that one over there?" Lawlor asked, pointing to an enemy with a grenade in his hand. "I'll bet ten p-notes I knock him off."

"With your M-60?" Lawlor's Viet counterpart asked derisively. "That's too easy."

"Hell, I'll kill him with anything you say."

"Anything?"

"Sure."

The counterpart thought it over. "A bedbug," he decided. "I'll bet you can't kill him with a bedbug."

"Catch him for me, and I'll do it for a hundred p-notes."

"Wait there," the counterpart said, leaving his hole.

Lawlor had knocked off three other NVA men by the time his Viet counterpart came back with the North Vietnamese soldier, a knife at his throat.

The ground below them practically swarmed with cooties. Lawlor picked one up with the help of a safety pin and turned to the soldier.

"Eat this bug," he demanded. "Go on, eat it."

The soldier looked sick, and even Lawlor's Viet counterpart was gray-faced.

"Eat it and we'll let you go," Lawlor said. "Refuse and you die."

The soldier reached out a grimy hand for the wriggling bug, put it in his mouth, and swallowed. Lawlor opened the man's mouth to make sure the cootie wasn't lodged someplace where it could be spit out afterwards.

"All right," Lawlor said, turning to his Viet counterpart. "You got all his weapons? Then let him go before he makes a mess around here."

The North Vietnamese was throwing up as soon as he stepped out of the hole, and he lurched back blindly toward his lines. At the speed he was making he was an easy target for one of the A team men. The North Vietnamese doubled up at the first bullet and was dead before he hit the ground.

"If not for the bedbug he'd never have lost control of himself like that," Lawlor shouted over to his counterpart. "That's a hundred p-notes you owe me."

"You were supposed to kill him *with* a bedbug," the Viet counterpart shouted back. "You cheated."

"He's dead on account of that bug," Lawlor insisted. "You owe me a hundred p-notes."

The enemy was mounting one of his human-wave attacks again, where two or three hundred would come charging at the concertina roll of barbed wire and the ones who lived would climb over it, every one of them shouting words like, "Yankee Die!" It was supposed to make a man's blood run cold, but the A team guys simply kept their aim careful and took more casualties than might have been the case otherwise.

It happened that way this time too. The enemy fell back finally, his dead on the other side of the barbed wire like ladders that could be used in the next charge.

Lawlor's Viet counterpart was dead too, a rifle bullet having finished him off. It upset Lawlor, even though he had already seen so many friends get it out here. He

219

cursed steadily during the first lull in the action. Then he climbed over into the next hole and rifled his dead counterpart's pockets of exactly one hundred piaster notes and nothing else. He was back in his own hole and shooting furiously when the next attack got underway.

Alex Birrell stood bent over the radio listening to Jerry Garfine say that more reinforcements were on the way and would get there in half an hour at the most.

Birrell said, "All right, Garfine, now get out there and hold out for half an hour."

Jerry Garfine smiled, grabbed for an M-16, and ran out of the tunnel and into fresh air tainted by the smell of death. Dac Hee Quang saw Birrell reach for a pair of grenades.

"Where are you doing, Captain?" he asked.

"Out."

Birrell discovered Jerry Garfine's body less than ten feet from the tunnel entrance. He planned on running over to one of the mortar crews and helping the men do their job, but he saw a dead Viet in a hole and an out-of-use M-60 in there with him. Birrell plumped down into the hole. He was next to Dave Lawlor. The sergeant's face was dark with sweat and dirt, but he grinned all the time.

"Nice to see you, sir," he shouted, although Birrell would have sworn that the man hadn't turned his head.

Birrell nodded his acknowledgement, but there was so much shooting all around them that he doubted if Lawlor noticed it. Enemy bodies were stacked like cordwood at the other end of the barbed wire.

Birrell shouted, "Who has an M-79?"

"Schmidt does, I think."

Birrell crawled out of the hole. He found Ken Hubbard with a busted M-60 and a grenade launcher. Birrell shouted out directions to Ken, and Ken fired grenades at the dead bodies piled up around the wire. The bodies

220

splintered into fragments, it seemed, and wouldn't be usable to the survivors as ladder steps to get them inside the base camp. One grenade struck a claymore mine, and the resulting sound was as loud as a bomb burst.

Birrell patted Hubbard's shoulder approvingly and started what turned out to be his round of inspection. He checked with as many soldiers as he could in order to find out how well they were doing and whether anything was needed. Time after time Alec Birrell crawled over to the QM emergency station for supplies and then crawled back to a given point with them. When he discovered a wounded soldier he'd call for the medic aid team, and in three cases he brought men to the dispensary himself. With Jensen and Wheeler both KIA, the dispensary was in charge of Viet personnel, who did their jobs quietly and quickly and well—up to a point.

There were too many dead bodies in the dispensary, and there wasn't any place to move them in a hurry. Birrell began lifting dead men under the armpits and moving them into the emergency map room. Dac Hee Quang looked offended, but he was shrewder than to argue with Birrell looking so determined during the course of an enemy attack.

Birrell went back to the men, hurrying as much as he could in order to get extra supplies. A burst of shrapnel nicked his right leg, and a bullet lodged itself in his left arm several minutes later, both apparently coming at him out of the blue. When Dave Lawlor tried to bring him back to the dispensary, Birrell shook his head stubbornly and kept moving.

His left arm felt as if it were being torn off at the roots while he worked. A bullet nicked him on the right side, causing so much blood to flow that he knew it was one of those flesh wounds that made plenty of mess but hardly ever did any lasting damage.

All the same it stopped him. He was on his way to the dispensary, when reinforcements landed by helicopter. He turned around, hoping to brief the captain in

221

charge of the new men, but fell on his face. One of the Viets had to carry him into the dispensary. A medic gave him something that put him to sleep.

He was in a hospital bed at Pleiku when he woke up again. Captain Quang came in to brief him after a med check, saying that the attack had been thrown back and that the enemy dead numbered seven hundred at least. The defenders had lost one hundred and forty men, including two helicopter crews and a medical evacuation team.

The men had done well, but Alec Birrell felt he hadn't done a damn thing. He had run his tail off while others did the fighting. He hadn't killed one enemy or wounded one, either. The action had been the biggest in which he had ever been involved, and his men deserved all kinds of honors for it; but he hadn't really done a single worthwhile thing to help them. He didn't talk much and couldn't bullshit with the rest of a team. He had never got through to them. They'd think of him as a goof-off, a runner, not the sort of leader who did things, who led his team in attacks or counterattacks.

He was still calling himself names when a telegram arrived for him. It had been signed by Ablett, Lawlor, Hubbard, and the other A team men who were still in good shape as far as he knew. The message, if that's what it could be called, was simply,

SO WHAT ELSE IS NEW?

They didn't have to insult him! Dammit, that was going a lot too far just because he had thought he could do more if he checked on the others instead of standing back of a—

And then Birrell understood. He took a deep breath in spite of the pain it caused him. The message was actually supposed to treat him as somebody who had been through a hard time along with the senders. They understood what he had tried to do. They liked him. They had accepted him with all his faults because they knew he cared

222

about them and was willing to put his life on the line in order to help. They liked him, they really liked him.

He held the telegram in his hand for three hours and put it to one side only long enough to finish a meal. When he went back to sleep, the telegram was in his hands again.

The last battle must have done the enemy considerable damage and put a crimp in his plans, because it took all of three weeks before he was able to mount another attack on the base.